The Five Flames Book 2

IN
SICKNESS

Kristina Circelli

A PERMUTED PRESS BOOK

ISBN: 978-1-68261-186-9
ISBN (eBook): 978-1-68261-187-6

In Sickness
The Five Flames Book Two
© 2016 by Kristina Circelli
All Rights Reserved

Cover art by Christian Bentulan

This book is a work of fiction. People, places, events, and situations are the product of the author's imagination. Any resemblance to actual persons, living or dead, or historical events, is purely coincidental.

No part of this book may be reproduced, stored in a retrieval system, or transmitted by any means without the written permission of the author and publisher.

PERMUTED
PRESS

Permuted Press, LLC
permutedpress.com

Published in the United States of America

*For everyone who heals the sick, no matter the darkness
that tries to keep you down.*

The Five Flames Series

Book One: Follow Me Home
Book Two: In Sickness
Book Three: Lie the Liar coming soon

PROLOGUE

The sun was lowering into a golden horizon when the spirit known as the Will O'Wisp made its way from the dark hallway to a front window on the first floor. Though it preferred the shadows, solid walls that hid it from prying eyes, it liked to watch the signs of life from the world outside. Every night, they came when the clock struck midnight—sometimes before, sometimes after, typically right on time. Usually the group was small, but some nights several faces peered up at the house that had seen far too many horrors.

Tonight was no different. A group of men and women stood across the street as one man gestured vividly, flashlight lighting up the front walk. It couldn't hear what was being said, but could imagine the stories. Little girls tied to chairs, children murdered while parents enjoyed a night on the town, strange lights luring wayward travelers, ghost hands on light switches.

And the most recent story—the woman named Tessa Taylor's mysterious haunting.

It didn't know the details, preferred not to know them, and tried desperately not to hear the whispers that occasionally made their way through the cloudy windowpanes. But one fact was clear: rumors were spreading about the woman's brush with the Savannah house, though, so far, no one had dared to discover the truth.

So the house sat empty, four angry spirits still trapped with their keeper. It felt their bitterness and understood it completely.

It, too, despised being caged here, and needed another brave, or perhaps foolish, soul to walk these walls.

And when that soul did come, the crimes committed by Tessa Taylor would be but a distant memory to the havoc it would wreak.

CHAPTER 1

The lab was quiet, too quiet, when he entered. The only light on was over the door, and there was no usual chatter of technologists and assistants as they prepared for a busy day. Just the cold metal tables, racks of empty tubes and syringes, and loose papers blowing lightly in the breeze of the AC.

Like a ghost town, he thought as he stepped forward, letting the door close behind him as he flicked on the rest of lights.

"The boss is back!"

Voices rang out from all around him, faces appearing just after. Jason Waters took a step back and hit the door, surprise apparent on his face. He watched as men and women poured in from all sides, all his work friends, lab assistants, and even a few hospital directors, appearing from behind storage cabinets and tables.

Laughter and conversation flowed from their happy faces. For a moment, Jason could only stare wide-eyed at the group before him, before he finally pushed himself off the door and limped forward. He sat in the rolling chair one of his techs offered him. While he had been cleared to return to work, he wasn't cleared for long periods of time on his feet.

It had been almost nine months since he'd nearly died at the hands of his former aide, his gut sliced open by a wayward blade concealed in a pant pocket. At the time he'd been sure he would die of the attack, and there were many days after he wondered how he was still alive, and wished that he weren't. Too many surgeries, too many nightmares...they were all too much for a body and mind cursed with a lifetime of pain. Though he technically was well enough to work, he still felt the nearly debilitating twinges of agony that reminded him how close to death he had been.

Shaking off those dark thoughts in favor of the lighter moment before him, Jason allowed a grin to form. These people had gathered here for him, and he would not deny them their moment. "Boss is back, everyone get to work!"

The collective chuckled, then began bombarding him with gifts and cake. Though it was entirely too early for sweets, Jason humored them, and let himself enjoy his first day back at the lab.

Later, when his team was mostly gone for the day and replaced by the usual skeleton crew, Jason took a moment to relax. In the quiet lab, with only the hum of analyzers surrounding him, he sat in his office and took in the familiar details.

There was his computer, with two monitors currently showing lab results he could read as easily as he could recite his phone number. There was the glass frog paperweight his niece had given him last Christmas, the only piece of fun décor in contrast to the framed diplomas and certifications on the walls. And there was a yellow sticky note next to his phone with the words he'd thought about every day for the past nine months:

Call me asap – RW

Glancing around and out the open office door, sure the lab wouldn't need him for a few minutes, Jason slowly pushed himself up from his chair and made his way out into the hall and to the elevator. It took him longer than he would have liked, as he was still under doctor's orders to do essentially everything as slowly as possible. Not that he would have gone against orders—even the simplest wrong move had pain shooting throughout his stomach and radiating up his spine.

In the elevator, Jason leaned against the wall, thankful that no one else got on during the ride up. He'd spent enough time trapped in a hospital bed, and later his own, having to rely on others to do nearly everything for him. Even as a child he'd hated letting people see any form of weakness, which was why he worked hard to keep his body strong and his mind sharp. But he'd had no defense against Tessa Taylor's attack, and the chaos it caused within him.

The elevator dinged, sounding his arrival. With a sigh, Jason pushed himself off the wall and began the slow walk to his friend's office, avoiding the stares of every nurse he passed. It was no secret what had happened to him—after all, he'd been treated in this very hospital—but he chose not to talk about it with most people, save his friend Roger Willcox.

"Figured you'd be hiding in here," Jason joked as he rounded the corner and knocked on the doorframe of a large office overlooking the St. Johns River. From the desk, Roger looked over and grinned.

"Jason! I heard you were back. I was going to come by the lab when I got off."

"Man, you've been coming to see me for months. About time I came to you." Jason waved him off with a laugh before sinking down in the chair on the other side of the desk. Thankfully, the chair was well cushioned, aimed for comfort, considering those who typically sat there were being delivered bad news.

He drummed his fingers on the armrest, glancing around at the cozy office, then turning his attention to his friend. Roger Willcox was an expansive man, with thick brown hair always perfectly styled and matching eyes that seemed a bit too big for his face. He towered over most people at six foot two, the extra pounds around his middle making him seem even larger. Some days he wore glasses, typically when he was particularly stressed or upset, which wasn't often. Jason had always admired how cheery the man was. He'd known Roger since his first year at the hospital, and respected the man's knowledge of all things medicine. He was convinced his friend was far more intelligent than he let on.

"Anyway," he continued, "I wanted to stop by and say thanks for checking in on me. I appreciated the visits, especially the snacks you snuck me."

Roger chuckled. "Don't let the big bosses know. Might revoke my license." He sat back, the chair squeaking beneath him. "How are you feeling?"

Jason shrugged and fought back a grimace. Currently, his stomach ached like he hadn't eaten in a week and he was exhausted. "Better. Still got a ways to go, probably a couple more surgeries to clear out all the scar tissue. But I'll live, which is what matters."

"And the nightmares?"

He hadn't told anyone about those, except Roger. Not even his primary physician or the hospital's on-staff shrink had been privy to that information. "Nearly every day," Jason admitted.

With a single, thoughtful nod, Roger stood and walked over to a long cabinet covering the entire far wall. He pulled a key out from his pocket. "I wanted to wait until you were back to show you this."

Curious, Jason slowly lifted himself from the chair and sauntered over to the cabinet. He knew what was in it—one side held a mini-fridge where Roger kept the snacks he didn't want anyone else knowing about; the other held a small deep freezer to store blood or plasma samples he was running his own tests on. When the freezer was opened, he couldn't see past Roger, and waited impatiently for his friend to turn.

Jason's eyes followed Roger's gaze down to his hand, where he held a small tube of blood wrapped in a blank yellow label. He didn't need to ask to know what it was. "How…"

"I found it in your kitchen, in the cooler, the day after you were attacked," Roger informed him, placing the tube back in the fridge and closing the door. "I had to believe that you were going to be okay, so I'd gone to get you some things for your stay and make sure everything would be okay at your place. When I saw this in that little lunchbox cooler in the fridge, I knew I had to keep it safe. I figured, doesn't hurt to keep it and see what we can find, right?"

A thousand questions came to mind, but Jason couldn't express any of them. Instead, he said, "I thought she had taken it. She erased the data you sent me. I figured for sure she'd get that as well."

"Maybe she's not as clever as she thought she was." Roger grinned, and it was a look Jason knew well. "I wanted to wait until you were healthy enough to handle this. I know what you're thinking: it's been months, and the sample is likely too far tainted to be of any use. That's why I took the liberty of running some additional tests just after I found the sample."

"And?"

That grin widened. "We have a lot to talk about."

CHAPTER 2

His home was dark when he walked through the front door, dark and empty and depressing. A year ago, he'd found his home to be just what he wanted—a nice, quiet space all his own where no one would bother him, with the occasional female companion. He'd never desired a wife, children, anyone who would take away from the time he wanted to and for himself. Now his home just felt vacant, and he'd come to realize that he almost wished there was someone else to greet him when he entered.

Ignoring his thoughts of self-pity, Jason made his way to his room, undressing along the way as he prepared for a shower. His reflection in the mirror made him pause. He no longer felt disgusted at the way he looked, just annoyed. Only a year ago, Jason had taken great pride in how he looked. He worked out four days a week, ate healthy meals, considered himself well-groomed.

Tessa Taylor had changed all that.

"*I don't need your help,*" she had snapped that fateful night, the voice coming from her lips tinted with a foreign accent that, at the time, he hadn't picked up on. "*You are just like them, and I don't need your pity. Get the fuck away from me before I do something we both regret.*"

She'd done something, all right, he thought wryly as he stared in the mirror. Two long, dark-red lines crisscrossed his abdomen where the concealed blade had sliced through his skin. She'd managed to cut through his lab coat and shirt to the flesh underneath, and he'd bled out on the hospital room floor while the doctors and nurses struggled to restrain the psychotic woman.

He didn't remember much of what happened next, but was told he'd died once on the operating table and been on the brink of death again for the better part of four days. In the end, he lost his spleen, a kidney that failed during surgery, needed several blood transfusions, and was left with a hell of a lot of pain and scar tissue. While he was trying to be okay with the scars, the pain was not something he was willing to get used to.

"I swear to God, if I ever get my hands on her..." he muttered to himself as he stepped in the shower. There had been talk of where Tessa and her delinquent brother were, but police were always a day late to the crime scene. It was like they were protected by magic, one newspaper claimed, two sociopaths murdering child abusers in the most brutal and elaborate ways, but no one ever saw them, or heard them.

They only discovered the aftermath.

As he did every night, Jason struggled to stop thinking of the woman who almost killed him. And just as he did every night, he told himself he would never stop trying to find out what had happened to turn Tessa into a murderer.

*

He met his old friend Roger at a local diner the next morning, just around the corner from the hospital. They sat at a booth facing the river, watching the sky welcome the morning sun in brilliant oranges and golds. A barge passed by slowly, crossing beneath one of the city's seven bridges, while smaller personal watercrafts began to fill the river, families out for a weekend of fun on the water.

It wasn't until their coffees and breakfast plates had been served that Jason finally asked why the doctor had requested the meeting. "You said you found something? I can only assume it has to do with the sample."

"It does."

"And it couldn't be discussed at the lab?"

After swallowing a mouthful of grits and eggs, Roger shook his head. "I think this conversation is best had away from any prying ears. But," he continued, forking up a serving of hash browns, "yes, it's about the sample and I'm hoping you have some answers, because I certainly don't. There's something…wrong with the sample."

"Wrong?" Jason repeated, brow furrowing. "What do you mean? Like it's expired? We already knew it was old, so I'd assume that time and taking it in and out of the refrigerator would—"

"No, no," Roger cut in. "I mean, yes, it's old, but that doesn't mean we still can't take a look around, see if we find anything unusual about it. No, I told you yesterday that I ran some tests back when the sample was fresh. As you said before you were attacked, Tessa was acting oddly. We couldn't find anything wrong with her physically. I'd suspected maybe she was on drugs, but there were no traces of any in her blood. So that left it something psychological, which is not my area of expertise."

Starting to get frustrated, Jason set down his fork, no longer hungry and just wanting to know what had Roger so out of sorts. He waited a moment to let his friend finish his next bite before asking, "What does this have to do with the sample?"

"Well," Roger swallowed a mouthful of eggs, "I decided to run some specialized testing for viral RNA, go a little deeper than the average test. I ran it a few times, before and after you were attacked, and there were…abnormalities."

Jason sighed. He was tired of the stalling. "Like what? Just tell me everything, Roger."

"I first noticed traces of a strange antibody in her blood, or what I first suspected was an antibody. I expected to see some, given that we thought she was sick, a cold or flu or the like. But I couldn't identify them." A long pause had both men nearly shivering in anticipation. "These foreign…factors. I've never seen them before. I ran a few different tests to try to isolate them and come to a conclusion on my own, but eventually had to go through years-old records to figure out what they were pointing to."

"And?"

Roger took in a deep breath, eyes dark and concerned. "Jason, all signs pointed to yellow fever."

Later, Jason looked over the results personally in his lab. They made no sense, but then, neither did Tessa's sudden departure into psychosis. He could almost accept something strange being found in the blood sample *because* of how much she changed in so short a timeframe. Yet, he was a man of science. There was an explanation to these results, and he was going to find it.

"Think, Jason," he ordered himself beneath his breath, staring at the computer screen and running a pen through his fingers, his way of trying to mentally work things out. "She went to Savannah, went on a ghost tour, had fun, came back feeling a little sick. Had some tests run, had elevated liver enzymes, crazy chemistries. Roger ran additional tests. Something is wrong with her blood."

His quiet mumbling got him nowhere, which elicited another sigh. He couldn't help but feel Savannah and the blood test results were connected, though not in the way the media was suggesting. Demon possession, a haunted house. Nonsense. There was no such thing as possession and no one would ever convince him otherwise.

"She doesn't even like the dark, so why the hell did she go on that tour in the first place," he mumbled, trying to connect pieces of the past. "Who cares why? She went on the tour, apparently broke into the Abercorn house and got herself possessed, kept going on the tour…Shit, forgot she cut herself on the tree." Remembering the bandage on her hand, he tried to recall if anything had ever come of it.

She'd been on the ghost tour, Tessa had said, and it was a stupid injury caused by leaning against a tree allegedly growing over bodies that died of yellow fever hundreds of years ago. He'd joked about her turning into a mutant, but never thought anything of it after that moment. Could it be possible, he pondered, for an actual mutation to occur...

"Get a grip," he muttered, throwing the pen down. "Get back to work."

CHAPTER 3

He spent the week mulling over the results, trying to figure out what they'd missed, what stone needed to be turned. But the sample continued to elude him. Roger was right—everything in the sample suggested Tessa's blood was harboring the yellow fever virus, except...not quite. There was something foreign about the results he couldn't understand.

By the time the next weekend rolled around, Jason knew what he had to do. He'd been in the field long enough, seen and heard enough about medical anomalies, to know that the best and fastest way to determine the root of a problem was to return to its source.

He had to go to Savannah.

Planning the trip took only one night on Google to find a hotel, and the name of the guide who had become famous since Tessa's fateful trip into that haunted house. He was somewhat eager to see the city that had supposedly been the place of Tessa's downfall. What he wasn't looking forward to was the long drive to north Georgia. Sitting for a few minutes was uncomfortable enough on his stomach; sitting for hours at a time was akin to torture.

But he made the drive anyway, stopping four times for a break from the pain, checking into the hotel to get situated and take a brief rest before continuing on his weekend quest. His hotel was located right on River Street, which he had planned purposely. Downtown Savannah was not an area for driving, but walking, and walking was something he did not want to do a whole lot of.

Setting out on foot, Jason got his bearings from the map he'd picked up in the lobby. Already he was regretting his decision to not bring the cane he usually needed to walk long distances. His feet moved slowly on the cobblestone road while his eyes took in the sights. The river to his right, shops of all types to his left, some kind of open market in front of him. He was looking for a kiosk or open office on the sidewalk, where he would find a ticket pickup counter.

After ten minutes of ambling about, stopping to let flocks of overexcited children race around the sprawling oaks, Jason walked up to the small kiosk, which was more like a shack along River Street. Only the faded sign nailed to the bamboo front told him he was in the right place—the ticket pickup for one of Savannah's most popular ghost tour companies. There was what he guessed was a teenager inside the hut playing on a laptop. "Excuse me," he said when he had come to a stop, leaning against the wooden counter.

The kid barely looked up as he replied with a brisk, "Yeah?"

Fighting not to roll his eyes or lecture the teen, Jason pushed on with his initiative. "I'm looking for one of your guides. I was hoping you could get me his contact information, or give him mine. His name is Augustus Jones."

"What do you want with Augustus?"

"Just to chat about his tours and get some information on the places he visits."

The kid glanced up, his boredom clear. "Why don't you sign up for a tour?"

Jason sighed and placed his business card on the counter. "Just give this to him, okay? It's important."

After the teen had agreed and placed the card next to his computer, Jason turned and began the long walk back to the hotel. Well, he mused, not a long walk by any means, but a slow one. While he was getting better at being able to stand and walk for longer distances, he still had to take it slow.

Just as he was contemplating stopping at one of the River Street restaurants for a break, he heard his name being called behind him.

Jason turned, seeing the man he'd previously only watched through the television screen, and waited until he'd caught up. "Yes?"

"Jason Waters? I'm Augustus."

"You caught up quickly."

Augustus lifted a shoulder at the not-so-subtle suggestion. "So I was around the corner, pretending I didn't hear the request to speak with me. I get a lot of people who want to talk to me about, well, you know. But then I realized who you were."

That wasn't a surprise to Jason. His attack had been highly publicized in the aftermath of the Taylor Sibling Slaughters. Not the catchiest name, he'd always thought, but it had been used once by a news anchor and stuck ever since. They'd tried interviewing him several times, finally giving up when he ignored them at every single attempt, but that didn't stop every news channel from plastering his picture everywhere. But others, like this Augustus before him, enjoyed the limelight and played up their parts in Tessa's story. Good for business, Jason assumed, when a ghost tour leads to a possession.

When Jason merely stared, the other man crossed his arms. "So why are you looking for me?" His voice didn't hold even a trace of the Irish lilt that was so prominent in his interviews, and during his tours.

His jaw set and shoulders square, Jason replied, "I want to talk to you about Tessa."

*

They walked silently to a nearby restaurant, sliding into a back booth and ordering a round of beers before getting down to conversation.

"You're going to ask me about the demon, aren't you?"

Surprised, Jason peered across the table. Augustus seemed genuinely interested, intrigued even. "You believe in all that?"

"No, but she did." Augustus sighed, thinking back to his meeting with Tessa and the friend who had tagged along. "She sat right there, you know, right where you're sitting, when she came back to see me. Asked questions about one of the houses she had broken into. Well, her friend did. For the most part she just sat there."

"Yeah, I know all that. You were more than happy to share with every news source out there."

"Hey, I was just answering questions," the guide said in defense. "If that fiancé of hers hadn't told the damn reporters that his bride-to-be thought she was possessed, it never would have come up in the first place."

"Unless you brought it up for him," Jason replied, already frustrated. "I don't care how the reporters found out or why she went into the house or whether or not she thought she was possessed or whatever else you two talked about. I want to know about your tour."

"That night?" Augustus shrugged and sat back. "Same as any other tour. Nothing out of the ordinary happened."

"Somewhere along the tour, Tessa cut herself on a tree. It wasn't a big deal; she probably didn't even mention it to you. But I don't know where. I want to know your route and the significant areas you point out."

"Because she cut herself on a tree? What's the big deal about that?" the guide asked. Jason only stared at him, his gaze so penetrating that the other man sighed and pulled a map out of his back pocket. He spread it across the table. "Fine. We started here, at the cemetery. I walked them around the corner and we stopped here." He pointed to an area on the map not marked by anything significant.

"What is it?"

"Honestly? Just an old concrete slab where kids used to play basketball. I always stop tours there because rumor has it, there are bodies buried beneath it. Yellow fever victims."

Jason's head snapped up, his attention peaked. "Yellow fever victims?"

"Supposedly," Augustus confirmed. "Savannah's got a nasty history with yellow fever; back in the late 1800s, it took out a good chunk of the population. They tried every old wives' tale in the book to cure it. Even burned tar in barrels along the streets thinking the smoke would help. Anyway, bodies were piling up, so they dug a trench and tossed 'em in. Like I said, rumor has it, this area is where some of those bodies can be found."

Ideas were spinning in Jason's head, but he kept them to himself. Too many ridiculous thoughts had formed that he knew to be impossible yet wanted to investigate nonetheless. "Does any vegetation grow there?"

"Sure. Some trees, a lot of weeds." Augustus narrowed his eyes. "Why do you ask? Doesn't have anything to do with the tree she cut herself on, does it?"

"Curiosity."

"Yeah, well, curiosity is what had that woman going into a haunted house. And look how that turned out."

Jason had been staring out the window as he thought, but now turned his blue eyes to the guide. "Can you show me the house, and the old basketball court?"

CHAPTER 4

They stayed long enough to finish their drinks, then headed out, beginning the slow walk to the cemetery. Twice Jason reminded the guide to slow down before giving up and leaving it up to him to realize how far ahead he was.

"She really did some damage, didn't she?" Augustus asked after the fifth time he'd looked back and had to stop.

"And then some." Jason wasn't interested in going into detail. His story had been told a hundred times over on the news the past nine months, a few specials even running using pictures shared by a friend or family member he still couldn't identify.

"Thought she was a little weird when I met her. Who breaks into a supposedly haunted house?" Augustus shook his head. "And then when she came back with her friend wanting to talk to me. I swear it was like there was nothing going on behind those eyes. Just a girl who wanted to fuck shit up and blame something other than herself."

Despite his crippling pain and the nightmares that would likely plague him for the rest of his life, Jason felt the sudden need to defend the woman who'd tried to kill him. "She was a good person, you know. Smart and kind. I don't understand what changed, why she did what she did, or is doing now. I guess I just wanted to see this all for myself, try to figure it out."

Augustus eyed Jason, remembering what he'd heard and seen on the news. The man was lucky to be alive, and been in the hospital for months. Every now and then the name Jason Waters appeared on a newsfeed somewhere, typically when another bloody and headless victim was found and suspected to be the work of one Tessa Taylor. "Sure, man. Get some closure. I get it."

They finally arrived at the cemetery. Jason glanced through the gate as they walked along its edge, finding beauty in the old tombstones and ornate mausoleums. He knew the cemetery had a dark history filled with stories of voodoo and animal sacrifices, but in the middle of the day, it didn't seem so bad.

"Here we are," Augustus said as they came to a stop on a cracked slab of concrete. He rocked on his feet as he reiterated the fact that yellow fever victims had been buried beneath the ground in mass trenches. Jason listened intently as he wandered around, occasionally kneeling to run his fingers along a crack in the slab or to touch one of the many weeds that littered the area. At the edge was an oak tree, its limbs sweeping toward the ground. He ran a hand down the rough-barked trunk, then peeled off a piece of that bark and stared at it in the palm of his hand.

Fingers closing over the remnant, he imagined Tessa walking in this exact place a year ago, on a ghost tour at midnight. She'd cut her hand here, possibly on this same tree, and brushed off the injury as just another cut. But *was* it just another cut? At the time he'd laughed it off as well; now he wasn't so sure.

Tucking the bark into his pocket, Jason turned to the guide. "Thanks for the tour. I'll head on to the house now."

*

He insisted on going alone, as much as Augustus insisted on going with him. As they walked to the house on Abercorn, the sun starting to lower as the afternoon wore on, Augustus filled him in on the background of the house. He started with the first death of the little girl tied to a chair and finishing with the last person to ever enter, that he knew of, anyway.

"I don't think anyone has been in since her," he told Jason honestly. "Maybe some cops or construction workers, since the place is all locked and boarded up now, probably to prevent the weirdos from seeing if they can solve the grand Taylor mystery. Some of the other guides will tell you they've seen things. Flickering lights through the windows, like fire. Others have claimed to have blacked out just from looking through the window. But I don't believe it."

"Not at all?"

Augustus stopped and turned to face Jason. "It's just a house, man. A house with a bad past that people want to make into something paranormal." Then he held out a hand and pointed. "We're here."

With a sense of dread, Jason allowed his eyes to follow the guide's finger and take in the supposed house of horrors. The residence loomed above him, two stories tall with a basement that opened at ground level, an expansive second-story balcony, a curved front staircase that was likely quite beautiful in its day, and concrete walls stained with time. The yard was filled with brown grass and bright green weeds, some growing in the shadows of wide-stretching oaks and dying banana trees.

But the dread he initially felt began to pass the longer he observed the home, now shadowed against an evening sky. Jason wondered what Tessa had felt when she first saw the place in the dark of night while being told ghost stories. Anxious, no doubt, maybe a little scared, with a chill down her spine. But Jason just saw an old, neglected house.

He took a step forward, only to be stopped by the strong hand that gripped his upper arm. Jason turned his head to see the guide staring at him incredulously. "What?"

"Where the hell do you think you're going?"

It was obvious to them both, but he answered anyway. "Where do you think? I want to see inside the place that supposedly turned Tessa into a monster."

"You can't go in there."

"Why? Because the cops put up some tape and a few boards?" Jason shrugged off Augustus's hand and continued up to the house. The sun had set now, and, being a weekday in the winter, the streets were fairly empty. He saw a car turn the corner up ahead and disappear, and a group of people down the sidewalk in the distance, but that was it.

Before Augustus could protest, Jason squatted down and tested one of the windows along the half-buried basement. He wasn't surprised when it creaked open. For some reason, he didn't imagine a house as old and abandoned as this one would have the best security measures in place.

When he was halfway through, he glanced back at the guide. "You coming?"

Though it was clear he didn't want to, Augustus followed. Soon they were standing in the cluttered basement with only the last glows of the sunset to guide them. Peering around, Jason saw what he considered a bunch of junk. An old bicycle in the corner, a table full of what were probably expensive antiques but to him looked like useless trinkets, boxes that were taped up and stacked, a few cracked wooden cabinets. And there, along the far wall, a set of stairs. He groaned inwardly, dreading the slow and painful walk up, but proceeded to them anyway, He relied heavily on the bannister until he reached the top.

"We shouldn't be here." Augustus's voice cut into Jason's concentration. "I could get fired for this."

"You don't need to go any farther. I won't be long. I just want to look around, anyway." Jason paused at the door and gave the guide a chance to leave, but he could tell the other man was curious. And, in the end, that curiosity won out.

The basement opened into the kitchen. By the light of his phone, Jason took in the dusty countertops and empty spaces where appliances once had been. The tile floor was cracked and covered with dirt, leaves, and trash likely left behind from other wayward explorers. Just off the kitchen was a small half bathroom, and what looked like a den or office on the other side of that. A narrow hallway separated the kitchen from the living room, which held a few pieces of furniture covered with white sheets, a small wooden coffee table, and a mantle above the fireplace with faded yellow photographs.

Standing in the doorway of the living room, Jason sighed, feeling both defeated and ridiculous. He didn't know what he'd been searching for, but was expecting *something*, some glimpse of what Tessa saw that fateful night. Instead there was just a dark house with dusty furniture and creaking wood floors. Nothing spectacular, yet nothing particularly creepy or unsettling, either.

He was about to turn to Augustus and suggest they head out when he saw it—a slight flicker of blurry light from a hallway to his left. For a few seconds he merely stared, watching as the lights became clearer. Four lights, he realized. Four floating candles. As his mind struggled to make sense of what his eyes were seeing, his feet began to move, drawn toward this mystery.

He shuffled through the living room and over to the hall, bracing a hand on the wall for support. Though his body was tired, the energy buzzing through his bones had him determined to figure this out. Fire didn't just float. Lights didn't appear out of thin air. His eyes latched on to those lights, widening as they came closer. In some part of his mind he recognized an outline of a figure attached to the lights, but so focused was he on the orange flickers before him that the thought of danger was but a momentary annoyance.

"Jason? Snap out of it, man!"

When a hand shook his shoulder roughly, Jason blinked a few times. He could feel his mind physically clearing as though a cloth were being wiped behind his eyes. "What?"

Augustus frowned and crossed his arms. "What the hell

are you doing? You were staring down the hallway like you saw something. I've been trying to get you back to earth for almost ten minutes."

Ten minutes? He'd just started walking down the hallway. *Did he see something in the hall? Lights, maybe?* He tried to remember what he'd been looking at, but the image was fading, and fading fast. Before he could feel concern for his sanity, it was gone completely. "Just...checking things out," he replied nonchalantly. "Come on. There's nothing here. Let's show ourselves out."

*

The figure at the window watched as the two men hurried away from the house, one thoroughly creeped out, the other glancing back curiously. The Will O'Wisp knew that look—it was the look of a soul caught in the inferno, not yet lost, but no longer walking a straight path. Soon the soul would realize the consequences of its curiosity.

For too many years now the Will O'Wisp had watched man and woman alike leave this house with that same look in their eyes. Curious, frightened, wary, accepting, bored, unbelieving, believing too much. They were always different, but met the same end. Just once, it wished there would be a soul strong enough to fight the claim. Maybe then, it would be free of this place, allowed to move on and leave the people of this city in peace.

It was a hopeful thought, followed by sigh.

CHAPTER 5

Jason arrived home annoyed and tired. He hadn't pushed himself that hard since the attack, and all the walking around, climbing in windows, and sitting for longer periods of time had worn his body out. He wanted a shower and bed and nothing else.

He reflected over his trip to Savannah as he washed himself, taking care around the scars on his stomach. Augustus had been pretty much what'd he been expecting—all theatrics—though he hadn't expected him to be quite so skeptical. At the very least he thought the man would believe some of the things he spoke about.

"So much for practicing what you preach," Jason mumbled with a quick roll of his eyes.

The house, well, he wasn't sure *what* he'd been expecting there. Something more…ominous, creepy, foreboding. Not just a house filled with crappy antiques. Though, he considered as he rinsed his hair, there were the four lights seemingly floating on air, but he chalked that up to letting his imagination get the best of him. Ultimately he could see why Tessa had been so afraid of her stroll through the house, given her fear of the dark, which might have even explained why she'd been so quick to assume her psychosis was a possession.

Stepping out of the shower, Jason walked over to the sink and opened the medicine cabinet, pulling out an orange bottle. After drying himself off and leaving the towel on the floor, he popped the top and dumped two pills into his hand.

He liked these pills. Not because he needed them for pain

or even to function during his waking hours, but because they prevented him from dreaming. For months he'd had nightmares, reliving the moment his stomach had been gutted open, his body collapsing in a pool of its own blood, everyone around him screaming in pain and fear. The pills made all that go away. He was trying to wean himself off them, but the nightmares just came back every time.

"Just fucking get rid of them for good." Downing both pills in one gulp, Jason crawled into bed and laid back, knowing it wouldn't take long before the medication would pull him into sleep.

*

He awoke in a world of black. Wondering if the power had gone out, as not even the clock on his bedside table offered its usual green glow, Jason carefully stood and began to feel his way out of the room. After he'd walked a few steps and his hand still hovered in the air instead of touching the wall, he began to worry.

He should have reached his nightstand three steps ago. The door to the bathroom should be right in front of him, outlined by the soft red glow of the cable box set along the same wall. But there was nothing. No table, no bathroom, no light to guide him. Just that gaping black hole and the rush of wind that rang in his ears. Even the carpet beneath his feet turned cold and hard, almost gritty, as though he were walking on wet sand.

It was then Jason realized he was still asleep.

An orange light began to glow in front of him. It was small at first, just a pinpoint of light in an otherwise empty world, and then began to grow. He took a few steps closer, gaze trained on that orb, until he was watching a movie of his life before him on a grand screen.

He saw himself as he used to be, able to move so easily.

Flashes of the man he once was—exercising at the gym, running along the beach at sunrise, enjoying the feel of a woman's body beneath his…those moments he had taken for granted, and even forgotten about, assuming he'd have many more. Then the screen shifted to a time he remembered far too well: getting off work late in the evening and moving into the patient room that would change everything.

"Stop," he whispered, willing his phantom self to turn around and walk away, to escape the horrible fate that awaited him. But he didn't, and Jason was forced to watch himself enter Tessa's room, talk to her. Though he couldn't hear the words, he mouthed them anyway, having memorized every part of that night, that final conversation, by heart. When she attacked, he felt it all over again—the fear, the pain, the acceptance of death.

He watched his body collapse, what looked like gallons of blood pumping from the wounds, bits of muscle and tissue and intestine peeking out through the raw folds of flesh. Bile rose in the back of Jason's throat. There was so much activity in the room—Tessa attacking the others with an almost inhuman strength—but his eyes were trained on his failing body. He'd never seen it from this angle before, and the sight infuriated him.

"You did this to me," he muttered, feeling that familiar rage boil to the surface. His attention shifted to Tessa when she stepped over him. There was no remorse on her face, no recognition of what she'd done. And oh, how he wanted to punish her.

"Such hate," said a voice behind him.

Jason spun, so startled it didn't even register that the move didn't cause him any pain at all. For a moment he could only stare at the…woman?…in front of him.

She was beautiful, in a hideous, terrifying kind of way. A sharp, angled face crafted by bone and shadow, matching an equally harsh body that lacked the softness of a woman's curves. But her body and face were of no matter to Jason, so fixated was he on the snakes coiled around her head. Snakes…instead of hair, he realized, swallowing hard.

Medusa? Jason wondered, and as if she heard the question in his head, the woman only cackled.

Finally he swallowed hard and found his voice. "Who are you?"

"I am the one they call Tisiphone," she replied, as though the answer should be obvious. When Jason only stared, she approached him, those coils shifting atop and around her head unnerving him. But he was frozen in place, unable to retreat when she reached out and drifted a hand across his shoulder, down his arm and back up like one may caress a lover. Indeed, he felt his body responding to her gentle touch, especially when her warm fingers grazed his chest, then lightly traced his scars.

"A shame," she whispered, regret in her beautiful voice, "such a shame to mar an otherwise beautiful specimen." Then her eyes, eyes so dark and full of fury, lifted to his. "You desire revenge for what was done to you."

It was a statement, not a question, one Jason didn't have time to refute before the screen in front of him changed.

Instead of his ripped-apart body writhing on the cold tile floor, he saw Tessa, on her back in his living room. Her clothes were torn and blood-stained, her eyes glassy, her throat colored with crushing bruises. One arm was outstretched, and he followed it, along with her glassy gaze, to see a second body a few feet away. Her brother, he realized, recognizing the pale, lifeless face that looked so much like its sister's. And there he was, sitting on the couch with blood literally staining his hands, staring down at the bodies like they were trophies waiting to be mounted on his wall.

Disgusted, Jason turned away from the vision. "What the hell is that?" he demanded. "I would never kill her, or her brother."

Confusion twisted the snake woman's face. "You would not seek revenge against the one who sought to kill you?"

The question made him hesitate. He'd never really thought about it before. He'd been so focused on dealing with the pain and recovering that actual *revenge* was never a consideration. It was easy to make off-hand comments about wanting Tessa to pay, but they were merely expressions of frustration. What would he actually do if Tessa appeared in front of him? Would he take it that far, to end her life?

The answer was simple enough. "Am I angry? Yes. Do I want her punished? Yes. But I don't want her murdered."

"I do not believe you."

The scene around them shifted, the screen fading into a gray background and a second figure emerging from the darkness to stand next to the snake-haired woman. This one was just as grotesque, though in an animalistic way, with a stork-like body and long beak, skin scabbed where feathers had been ripped from its body.

Before Jason could speak, the creature lurched forward, nails dragging in the ground beneath him to form a triangle. "Lie to the ones who hold your soul, choke on the truths you refuse to speak."

Rather than frighten or intimidate, the remark only succeeded in confusing Jason. "Uh…what? I'm not lying about anything."

Tisiphone pointed at him. "You want revenge against the one who crippled you. You *need* revenge. And now you will speak the truth, so my brother in the shadows and I may fight for our just reward."

He heard the desperation in her voice, wondered why she was so determined to hear him say the words she tried to prompt out of him. "I…I don't want revenge against Tessa, because I care about her," he answered honestly. "I don't know what happened to her to make her do this, and become some kind of serial killer, but *something* happened. I want her to get the help she needs. I don't hate her. I'm sad for her."

Hearing himself say the words out loud, Jason realized then

just how much he meant them. He really did care about her, not romantically, but as a friend, a young woman he'd worked alongside, hoping she would one day take his place. Knowing that he didn't hold any hate for her eased some of his anxiety.

But it didn't ease Tisiphone's. She pressed her lips together, annoyance and sorrow crossing her eyes before she nodded once. Her hands withdrew from his body, but one finger traced his chest in an X. "There is sickness in your heart," she whispered, one bitter glance back at the stork beast behind her, "but only one can cure it. We are not the ones your soul craves."

This time, when he woke, it was back to the reality he knew.

CHAPTER 6

The dream—nightmare? —haunted Jason in his waking hours. He mulled over it on the drive to work, wondering who the snake-haired woman was, why the bird creature had drawn him in a triangle and ordered him to speak the truth, and even more over his confession about Tessa. As he thought about it, he accepted his dream self had told the truth. He really didn't hate the woman who tried to kill him.

That revelation followed him into the lab, encouraging him to lock himself away in the back room with the specimen refrigerator. Tessa's blood sample still sat in a red biohazard bag on the rack, where he'd placed it to be thawed after taking it from Roger's deep freezer. Removing the bag, he made quick work of separating the sample into two parts. One went back into the refrigerator, the other into a petri dish he set inside a small incubator.

Jason stared at the sectioned-off sample through the glass for a moment, eager to see what would happen when a little heat was added and thinking back to his trip to Savannah, forcing out thoughts of the flickering lights in favor of what Augustus had told him about the yellow fever victims.

Buried in mass graves, he'd said, trenches without headstones that would later be covered by pavement. Bodies some say were later moved to real graves, but others claim were left to rot, their blood and organs and flesh seeping into the earth that surrounded them.

Could it be possible? Jason pondered as his eyes roved over the seemingly innocent-looking petri dish. The idea had been floating around in the back of his mind since he drove back to Florida, and though it was one that normally he would have laughed off as being the plot of some B-list horror flick, now he was willing to give it serious consideration.

Viruses didn't typically live long outside the body. Twenty-four to forty-eight hours, at most a week. Yellow fever was a virus, spread by the bite of mosquitos. But, he continued with his outlandish train of thought, what if the virus mutated and found a new way to spread? What if it seeped into the ground via the victims' blood, those mass graves now part of the earth, part of the vegetation that drew its life source from the soil? Could it be possible for a virus to lie dormant within that vegetation, waiting for the moment when it would come in contact with a new host?

Tessa had cut her hand on a tree that grew atop unmarked graves of yellow fever victims. Was it possible that, somehow, the virus had entered her bloodstream?

"And, at the very least, it turned her insane," Jason murmured. His eyes narrowed at the thought. There was no denying that *something* strange had happened to Tessa, but virus-by-oak-tree seemed far too much a stretch. Besides, she never showed any symptoms of yellow fever. Though, he considered, the virus could have mutated, taking on new symptoms, such as psychosis.

Jason shook his head, annoyed with himself for entertaining such thoughts. "You are losing your goddamn mind," he muttered.

"Am I interrupting?"

Startled, Jason spun around, inwardly cursing himself for the rapid movement when his gut clenched. He fought not to show pain as he took in the sight of the woman before him. She was young, perhaps early twenties, with chestnut-red hair that fell in curls down her back, the brightest green eyes he'd ever seen, and a sprinkle of freckles across her nose.

He wanted her immediately. Something basic and carnal stirred within him the more he took in that gorgeous face complemented by a curvy body dressed in a pair of tight black pants and white button-up blouse. "Can I help you?"

If she noticed he was in pain, or that he was eyeing her like a meal, she showed no recognition. Instead the woman only smiled, the grin lighting up her perfectly adorable face. "My name is Clara. Um...today is my first day with your lab?"

She sounded unsure, which only made her even more desirable. Jason cleared his throat. "You were hired recently?"

"A few weeks ago," Clara replied, clasping her hands in front of her. "They wanted me to start after you returned, so you could show me the ropes and meet the new person in your lab. I was hired as one of your medical technologists."

He didn't have the best luck with techs and phlebotomists, considering the disaster with Tessa, but he was willing to take a chance on this one. "Well, it's nice to meet you, Clara. I'm happy to welcome you aboard."

"More than happy to be on board, sir."

The slight tease in her voice had Jason hesitating, wondering if he'd heard her correctly. "Give me a few minutes to finish up in here, then I'll show you around."

She shot him another one of those thousand-watt smiles before nodding. "That sounds great. I look forward to everything you can teach me."

Now he knew he was hearing something between the innocence of those words. "As do I, Miss Clara," he replied, his voice low as he tested the waters of what he guessed was flirtation with a woman he'd only just met.

Then she left him alone, and Jason released the breath he hadn't realized he was holding. It took him a moment to clear his thoughts and remind himself that no matter what he instantly felt for the woman, she was his new employee, which made her off-limits. It pissed him off that the first time since his attack he'd felt well enough to act on those feelings of lust, he wasn't able to do a damn thing about it.

With a sigh, he looked back at the incubator and grabbed a black covering, ready to hide the rack away from the rest of the world again. He started to turn away from the blood sample, but a slight flicker of movement caught his eye. Brow furrowed, Jason narrowed his eyes as he observed the petri dish on the shelf. The breath whooshed from his lungs when he saw the bubble that had formed in the center of the serum.

His eyes widened, taking in that single boil, blinking when it popped, only to form again. The blood rippled and swirled, creating tiny boils that built into those bubbles reaching for the edges of the plastic casing that confined them. He clenched his hands into fists as he realized the sample, in the heat of the incubator, had become a living, thriving organism, all but demanding its freedom.

But what kind of organism, Jason had no idea. He'd never seen this kind of activity before, this kind of growth, especially in a sample that should, logically, be absolutely worthless. And so when he spoke, his voice was but a whisper filled with terror.

"What have we done?"

*

Jason paced nervously in the back room of the lab, hands clasped behind his back while he waited for Roger. He'd quickly forgotten about his promise to show Clara around in favor of having a conversation with the doctor—an immediate conversation. It seemed over an hour passed before the doctor finally turned away from the microscope, though it likely was only ten minutes.

"So what do you think?" he asked when Roger looked over at him, concern etched across his face. "Not normal, right? I've never seen a blood sample react this way."

"Not normal?" Roger repeated with a sarcastic laugh. He ran a hand through his thinning hair. "Jason, this is…I can't explain it."

"You have to," the other man insisted. "You are the smartest doctor in this entire damn hospital. If you don't know why we're seeing blood, what, boiling? Then who the hell can? I need answers."

"Jason, I'm a doctor. I deal with facts and figures and data. I don't know how to explain blood samples all but coming to life in front of my eyes. This," he gestured a thick hand to the sample behind him, "this is dangerous. The sample needs to be destroyed, immediately."

"Destroyed? You were the one who insisted on keeping the sample all these months and doing more tests behind the board's backs."

Roger nodded, hesitation spread across his face. "I know. I was. But now…something doesn't feel right, and I'm not looking to lose my job or my license for something potentially dangerous. It was an interest at first. Now it's a concern. It needs to be destroyed."

Even though he agreed with his friend, Jason felt his temper flare immediately at the suggestion. The sample *did* need to be destroyed for their safety as well as everyone around them, but, for some reason, it angered him that Roger would dare say such a thing.

He envisioned himself grabbing hold of the doctor by the back of the neck and slamming his head down on the table, enjoying the sickening crunch of bone against metal, salivating against the scent of fresh blood dripping to the tile floor. Another human being defenseless against his strength and cunningness, unable to protect himself in the face of his fury.

That sudden burst of rage frightened Jason enough that he took a step back and braced himself against the counter. "You're right," he said after a moment in as controlled a voice he could manage. "I'll destroy it immediately."

"See that you do." Trusting his longtime friend, Roger patted Jason on the shoulder before seeing himself out, eager to get away from the unexplainable specimen.

Alone in the small room once again, Jason resumed pacing, considering his options. He could destroy the sample. Ten percent bleach solution mixed into the tube containing Tessa's blood, a few shakes to mix it up, and there would be nothing left to worry about. The sample would be just another tube tossed in the biohazard bin.

It would be for the best. It would be the *right* thing to do. But he didn't want to do the right thing. He wanted to take it a step further, see what he could create.

And while that fact scared the hell out of him, it also gave him a sick kind of thrill.

It was no secret Jason had always had an obsession with diseases, viruses, bacteria. An almost unhealthy obsession, some might say. He loved reading about plagues, researching the spread of viruses, watching the effects illness had on the body. It was the reason why he wanted to work in a lab, surrounded by samples of blood containing the best and worst of illnesses. And, right now, he wanted to know all about this sample.

"Be a shame to destroy it," he murmured. His eyes locked onto that petri dish, the blood cultured onto the media with its red coating and mysterious bubbles. There was so much they could learn from this sample, so much science, medical phenomena, waiting to be unveiled. He could be the first to map the spread of a virus not through blood or air of fluid, but by the roots of the very earth itself.

His hand reached out, fingers dragging down the glass of the incubator door, as he uttered the words that, later, he wouldn't remember speaking. "You will be my greatest experiment."

CHAPTER 7

He finished up his work on a high, his mind already working through the possibilities of his medical breakthrough. There was still so much work to do—travel back to Savannah and take samples from the site, thoroughly research yellow fever, run additional tests on the sample—all without letting anyone know what he was actually doing. He didn't think the scientific community as a whole, not to mention the hospital administration, would support his experiment.

So he would work in secret, letting Roger think the sample was destroyed, and continue his work until he'd reached a point that it could be shared.

Jason left the lab once the night shift had arrived, forgetting until he closed the door behind him that he never helped Clara on her first day. He hoped one of the other techs had taken her under their wing, and made a mental note to apologize to her first thing tomorrow morning. As he drove home his thoughts turned back to Tessa's blood sample, but by the time he stepped into his house he was no closer to figuring out how he would even proceed with his tests, let alone determine any sort of conclusion.

Exhausted, and irritated that one day of work left him so tired and in need of a damn bed, Jason made quick work of grabbing a bite to eat before shedding his work clothes in the bathroom. Remembering last night's dream, he downed three pills instead of two, hoping to black out and avoid another nightmare of some crazy demon who claimed sickness lived in his heart. He'd been tempted to Google the snake woman, see if there was some truth to his nightmare, but he was a scientist, not a dreamer. What visions he saw when his mind drifted into nighttime oblivion were merely the work of an imagination rarely given the opportunity to go beyond the scientific.

Once in bed, it took him a few minutes to find a comfortable position, and another few to realize sleep was not going to happen despite the pills. His mind was too amped up on the possibilities of the blood sample and the virus that lived within it. With a sigh, he threw back the covers and slipped on a pair of sweats before heading to the kitchen.

The clock on the stove read ten PM. Jason nearly rolled his eyes at himself. "Ten o'clock and you're out of bed not able to sleep," he muttered, remembering a time when he could stay up all hours of the night. He grabbed a beer from the fridge and sat at the counter, intending to do a little research, then jumped when the sound of knocking interrupted the otherwise quiet house.

"What the hell?" He turned, surprised to realize the sound was coming from the front door. That surprise deepened when he saw who was on the other side. "Clara?"

The new phlebotomist smiled shyly at him and shuffled her feet. "Hi, Mr. Waters. I went to the movies after work and was on my way home and…well, we weren't able to speak earlier when the doctor came to visit, and…I was hoping—"

"How did you know where I lived?" he cut in, more confused by that than why she was there, late at night, no less.

Her feet shuffled again. "Um…I saw your address on one of the files."

"Is everything okay at the lab?"

"Yes."

"Then why are you here?" He stared at her for a moment, and when she looked up at him with those sea-green eyes, realization dawned on him. He nodded and stepped back. "Come on in."

He led her to the living room, doing his best not to limp. He knew why she was here. There was no reason why a pretty, young lab aide would stop by his house after her first shift at his hospital unless she was interested in him as more than a boss. Usually he would have turned her away, citing professional behavior and whatever other regulations came to mind, but now, after the discovery of a potentially new virus, he was feeling a little more confident.

And, let's be honest, he thought wryly, *it's been a while since a woman looked at you like she just did.* Yet another thing Tessa had taken from him.

So he would enjoy this night, whatever came of it, and deal with the consequences in the morning.

"Can I get you a glass of wine?" he asked. She nodded, so he made quick work of pouring a glass of red and handing it to her, settling down on the couch next to her with a beer of his own.

"So today was your first day," he stated the obvious, trying to think of something to lead them into conversation. "I apologize for leaving you hanging. I needed to meet with someone to discuss a test we have been running. I hope you were able to get started smoothly."

"Oh, yes," Clara assured him, one hand tucking back a lock of thick red hair. "Your techs were really helpful and showed me around."

"Good." With a nod, Jason sat back and ran an arm along the back of the couch. "Since I didn't get to interview you, tell me a little about yourself."

Clara took a sip of wine. With her attention momentarily diverted, Jason allowed himself to look her over. Long hair curling down her back, pale skin already a bit flushed from the wine, soft yellow shirt hugging the curve of her breasts. She had changed from what she was wearing at the office, and he was glad for it. Only when she lifted her eyes to his did he attempt to appear like he wasn't just imagining her naked.

"Okay, well…I'm twenty-two. Um, I graduated recently and moved to Jacksonville from Tampa. I have family here and wanted to be close to them. I've always been interested in medical things, especially how bacteria and viruses affect the body. I thought about becoming a doctor or some sort of researcher, but, to be honest, I didn't want to go to school that long." The smile she shot him was sheepish. "So I decided to become a phlebotomist. Let's see, what else. Um…I am a big fan of classical music, and I absolutely hate camping."

Jason laughed, not able to imagine this delicate specimen in the middle of the woods next to a campfire. "I'm not much of a camper either," he admitted, though he wouldn't admit that really he didn't care for it because he wasn't a big fan of having to do all the manly shit, like starting fires and putting up tents that were always a pain in the ass. "Though I do enjoy hiking."

"I imagine you're quite at home with anything sports related. You seem very fit."

"I used to be." He regretted saying the words, not wanting to turn the conversation from flirtatious to pitying, but there was no taking them back now.

"I remember hearing about your attack on the news," Clara admitted, her formerly flirty eyes downcast, settling on his hands, which were wrapped around the beer in his lap. "I remember being so disgusted with that Tessa woman. Such a terrible thing."

Attempting to appear nonchalant, Jason lifted a brow. "I guess. But I'm alive, so that's something to celebrate. Try not to live in the past, you know?"

"I agree. To living in the now." Clara clinked her glass against his beer with a soft chuckle. "I have to admit though, when I heard there was an opening in the lab after all that settled down, I wanted to be one of the first to apply."

"Why?"

She shrugged, an innocent, girly shrug. "I guess I figured,

maybe I'd get to meet you, if you came back to the lab. And...that probably not a lot of other people would want to apply, given what happened at the hospital, so I was more likely to be hired. I really needed the job."

Her honesty charmed him, both revelations. Spurred on by the way she crossed her legs and shifted closer to him on the couch, Jason reached out and drew a finger down her cheek. "Looks like you got what you wanted, on both accounts."

She peered up at him, a small smile playing at the corners of her mouth as she whispered the word he accepted as an invitation: "Almost."

With that he took her lips, parting them with his tongue, tasting the sweet tang of wine. He set his beer on the coffee table, pulling the wine glass from her hands to do the same. Once their hands were free they moved them to each another, one exploring the feel of the man she'd admired from afar, the other enjoying the soft curves of a woman who was willing to let him do as he pleased.

And so he did, yanking the shirt from her body, letting his eyes bask in the sight of her large breasts spilling out of a white lace bra. They filled his palms as he kissed them one at a time, his mouth working its way up to her throat, where he felt the hard beat of her heart, and back to her lips, from which raspy moans sounded as music to his ears. Her skin burned against his.

"Jason," she whispered his name, sliding a hand between them to massage him through his jeans. His mouth broke away from her jaw with a groan and he shifted, giving her better access. She tried to tug at his shirt but he refused, not wanting his ugly scars to ruin the moment. So instead she tugged at the button of his jeans and freed him, his warm hand wrapping around him in soft strokes that had rough grunts shuddering from his body.

"Jason," she whispered again, her grip tightening, "take me."

He opened his eyes, surprised to find her staring back at him. All traces of innocence had vanished, replaced by something primal and wild and filled with desire—and he was ready to fulfill that need. He wasn't going to ask if she was sure, wasn't going to stop and wonder if he was making a mistake, if this was all happening too fast. No, he was going to take her, right here, right now.

The skirt she wore was pushed to her waist, her thong to her ankles, and then he was on top of her. In one fluid move he thrust into her, the feel of her tight and wet as both of them moved together.

Jason felt her legs wrap around his waist as he kissed her, one hand sliding behind to grip the back of her neck. He barely acknowledged her fingers digging into his shoulders, or her gasps of pleasure, as he rocked into her as deep as he could go. What he did notice was the taste of copper that hit his tongue.

He pulled back, a garbled curse escaping his lips when he saw the blood spread on her mouth and chin.

"Shit, Clara." He attempted to rise, but she protested. "Clara, you're bleeding." It pained him to pull out of her and sit up, but he did, tugging her up with him. He grabbed a wad of tissues from the coffee table and wiped at her face. "I just need to see where it's coming from and I'll stop the bleeding." It was then that he noticed just how hot her skin was. What he'd mistaken as lust and desire earlier was something far more serious; she was feverish.

"Clara, you're sick. You're burning up."

"I'm fine," she insisted, taking the tissues from his hands and throwing them to the floor. She shoved him against his shoulders, and the shock of the move, combined with her surprising strength, had him flat on his back on the couch. Clara crawled on top of him, and before he could protest, she had lowered herself onto him again with a gasp, both of them moving together.

"Clara," Jason groaned out, hands gripping her hips as his pelvis thrust against her almost against his will. "Clara, you need—"

The vision before him silenced Jason. Clara sat atop him, eyes closed in ecstasy, blood seeping from the corners like tears. Thick red liquid created two rivers down her cheeks, melding with the smudges he'd created on her jaw. More blood dripped from her nose, and he traced the path with his eyes—over those full lips, down her chin, until finally landing on his shirt. He opened his mouth to protest but she silenced him with a finger to his lips, a red-hazed grin forming on her pretty face, which had become a mask of blood rivulets that he stared at in horror.

But she continued to ride him and he let her, fascinated by this feverish woman, sick desire curling in his gut at the sight of blood, until he felt his release deep inside her so hard and fast it jolted his entire body.

Jason shot up in bed, heart pounding against his chest as he struggled to regain his senses and surroundings. His breath heaved out of him in thick gasps until he was clutching his stomach in pain. It wasn't until his heart finally slowed that he realized he was alone in his room, and that his time with Clara had just been a dream.

Didn't feel like a dream, he thought as he took stock of his situation. His shirt and sweats were on the floor and his bedspread was tangled around his legs. His body certainly felt primed for sex, and he couldn't deny the satisfaction that had him craving a nap.

Forcing himself out of bed, Jason stumbled into the bathroom for a quick drink of water, glancing at himself in the mirror. He looked haggard and exhausted, and a little panicked. With a grimace, he returned to bed, convincing himself it was just a dream, that while he may have been attracted to the cute new employee, he could never act on it in person.

But the way his desire presented itself worried him. Was he fascinated by illness? Yes. Did it turn him on? He'd never thought so before. But he couldn't deny he'd enjoyed the blood-fueled sex with Clara. More than enjoyed it—his body wanted more.

"Stop it," he muttered to himself. "Just a sick dream." But curiosity had him retrieving the clothes from the floor, and fear had him freezing in place as he looked down at the items in his hands.

There, in the center of the shirt, were three drops of blood.

*

The Will O'Wisp had seen many men like Jason before. Those who didn't believe, who preferred fact over fancy. Those who, deep down, *wanted* to believe. Those who took curiosity as far as it would go, even if it destroyed them.

It watched in its mind's eye as Jason woke from his dream, only to question what was real after all. The mortal man fought fancy at first, willing to write off a dream of sickened passion as merely the work of a troubled mind, but then he saw the evidence of such a dream. Suddenly fantasy wasn't so impossible after all.

It surprised the Will O'Wisp, how easy this soul was to conquer. For such a scientific mind, Jason Waters was susceptible to the suggestions his demon was already sending to him in sleep, and predicted it wouldn't be long until the man had willingly given himself over…perhaps all for the sake of science, or even for the touch of a beautiful woman.

Yes, the Will O'Wisp had seen many men like Jason before. And it had seen many men fall.

CHAPTER 8

He went into work late the next day, needing a little extra time to compose himself after last night's all-too-real dream. Jason was still trying to sort it out as he drove to the hospital and headed into the lab.

The dream he could explain. He hadn't had sex in a while, and there was no denying Clara was attractive. And they'd enjoyed mild flirtation during their first meeting in the lab. So, maybe he did have a little interest in her. Her suddenly hemorrhaging while he was thrusting into her and continuing like she didn't even notice? That one he couldn't quite figure out. And the blood on his shirt, in the same place where Clara's blood had dripped onto him in the dream.

A nosebleed, he considered as he slowly walked the hall to the lab. A nosebleed while he slept that maybe he wiped on his shirt, and it manifested itself in his dream.

Satisfied with the explanation, he pushed open the lab door and greeted the few employees sitting at the counters behind microscopes. He paused when he saw Clara perched at her desk. "Clara," he said softly, nodding at her and hoping his voice didn't betray the dirty thoughts racing across his mind as it took him back into his dream.

"Mr. Waters," she said just as softly. He noted the way she crossed her legs and licked her lips, averting her eyes as he passed. His gaze never left her until he was in his office and he could analyze her reaction. She'd seemed shy, almost embarrassed. Briefly he entertained the idea that she'd had just as tantalizing a dream about him last night as he'd had about her, but then he laughed to himself and got to work.

The time for absurd thoughts was over.

He checked on the sample first, making sure he was alone in the back room before pulling down the cover and sliding over a few useless petri dishes he'd tucked in front of the one he really wanted to see. Disappointment filled him when he gazed upon Tessa's blood sample only to find no significant changes. No growths, no bubbles, no color changes. Just the sample, and all the mysteries it contained.

His curiosity settled for the time being, Jason left the room. The lab was empty, his techs all out doing their daily jobs, save for the woman still at her desk. *Shit.* He'd forgotten about the new girl again. "Clara?" he said as he approached her. She looked up at him with those amazingly green eyes and smiled. "I'm sorry for not being able to show you around yesterday. I hope one of the techs took care of you."

"One of them showed me around, yes," she replied, her voice soft and sweet. "Though I was hoping you would take care of me today."

Forcing himself to pretend like he didn't hear the not-so-subtle suggestion in her reply, Jason nodded and gestured with his head. "Let's take a tour."

She rose to her feet. "Before we begin, Mr. Waters, I just wanted to say that I'm sorry for what happened to you. The attack and all. I followed your story on the news and it's actually why I wanted to work here. I figured someone who could survive that and have the courage to come back to the same place where it happened was someone I wanted to work for."

A bit taken aback, Jason paused before replying, "Well, thank you, that means a lot. But I don't really like talking about it, so... let's get back to the tour, shall we?"

He led her around the lab, pointing out the storage room and where she'd get her supplies for her daily sticks, the break room with its long list of rules for eating in and around a lab, the general workstations, and the back room where most of their more intricate analyzers were housed.

"We keep the tubes organized in these racks," Jason placed a hand next to a blue rack with twelve sections that each currently held a labeled tube, "and sort them according to what test we're doing or what machine is being used. The biggest thing is to always make sure you keep your samples organized. We can't have things going missing or tests being late or anything like that. Organization is key to the lab."

"Got it," Clara said solemnly, her red hair framing her face and giving her a somber look.

"You might have seen a handful of these machines during school, but anything you don't know, we'll make sure you're up to speed. Most of them are pretty easy. Go ahead and take a few minutes to look around, and let me know if you have any questions."

Leaning back against the counter, Jason let Clara wander around the room. He watched her observe each machine, each rack of blood—and there were many. Her expression was one of curiosity and excitement as she took in each piece of equipment, and he imagined her mentally taking notes and filing away questions to ask later.

"What do you think?" he asked after five minutes had passed.

She stopped her perusal a few feet away from him, one hand trailing along the metal countertop. "I think I can't wait to get started," she answered, biting down on her bottom lip. Jason's eyes locked onto that lip as he imagined taking it between his own teeth.

"You don't get squeamish around blood, right? I know it sounds crazy to ask, but I've had techs before who thought they could handle it and ended up passing out in rooms like this."

Clara shook her head, a ghost of a smile toying on those full, painted lips. "No, of course not," she laughed. "To be honest, I find it all a little...thrilling. Maybe I shouldn't admit that."

At her self-conscious smirk, Jason had to chuckle. "No judgment here. It's common knowledge around here that I'm somewhat fascinated by diseases, illnesses, what have you. Morbidly obsessed, according to some people."

"Well, then we have that in common. It's rather sexy, in a way, being surrounded by the very life force of our bodies." Clara took a step forward, one finger tracing a path on the counter. Her sudden shift from shy to confidence unnerved Jason, and he cleared his throat to avoid doing something that might get him fired.

"All right, well, that wraps up the tour. I'll have you shadow one of the techs for the next week or so until you're comfortable with the routine, then make you up a schedule of your own."

"I think you are going to do something great."

The statement seemed to come out of nowhere. Though Jason was aware the young woman was clearly flirting with him, he did his best to remain professional. "I appreciate that, Clara. So—"

"I think you could use your experience and this incredible lab to create something the world has never seen before," Clara cut in as she looked around the room. "Make a breakthrough in the medical community, and be hailed a hero."

Though his mind raced with how the conversation had turned, Jason couldn't deny the ego that inflated at her admission. He imagined himself doing that great thing, and he knew just how to do it, once given the time and motivation. Everyone would know his name; everyone would *celebrate* his name. History would remember him as the man who discovered a new way for viruses to travel—and the way to cure them.

The sample was only a few feet away in the rack at Clara's back. He looked over at her, wondering if she knew what he'd been thinking, then chastised himself. She was just a new, young tech with big aspirations, and what better way to accomplish them than by buttering up the boss?

Determined not to be taken with her, Jason cleared his throat again and turned. "Let's get you settled in."

The inflated sense of self and ego followed Jason home. It was as though he could hear the sample calling to him, pleading with him to be free, as Clara's words echoed in his head.

"You could use your experience and this incredible lab to create something the world has never seen before...be hailed a hero." He didn't care that she was merely trying to suck up to him. Her words struck that part of him that desired, craved, lusted for more than what he had.

And what he craved was the power to create something the medical world had never seen before.

So excited he was by the prospects of his near future that he cooked a full and hearty meal, one of his first real attempts in the kitchen since the attack. Not that he'd ever been much use in there before, but he'd learned a few bachelor tricks over the years and could put together a decent menu when the situation called for it: a juicy steak, side of mashed potatoes, and fresh green beans. He sat at the kitchen counter while he ate, staring straight ahead at the wall while he chewed, his mind racing with possibilities.

The ringing of his cell phone jarred Jason out of his thoughts. He looked down, surprised to see his plate was empty, then pulled his phone from his pocket. Roger's name glowed on the display. "Evening, Roger," he greeted warmly.

"Jason," the doctor said in return. "I was just calling to check in, see how you were feeling now that you've been back at the office for a bit. Do you need anything? Feeling okay?"

"Feeling fine," Jason replied honestly. "A little pain here and there, but I know my limits."

"Avoiding your usual late nights and early mornings?"

Jason chuckled, memories taking him back to a time when he

would have eagerly done such long hours. It had even become a sort of running joke in the lab, techs taking bets on whether he'd be in the same clothes when they started their next shift. More often than not, they won.

"No long nights or early mornings," he answered his friend. "Truth be told, I'm lucky if I'm still awake past nine o'clock these days. But overall, but I think I'm doing pretty well. I appreciate the offer though. I do want to take you out for drinks someday soon, as a thank you for all your help this past year."

"Not necessary." Roger paused, then added, "So did you get rid of the sample?"

Annoyance rose to the surface at the rapid change in conversation and clear understanding as to the real purpose of this call, but Jason pushed it back so his voice was clear when he answered, "It's no longer a concern."

"Good, glad to hear it."

Before Roger could continue his line of questioning, Jason changed the subject. "Do you happen to know who took over the interviews and hiring while I was gone? There is a new tech that just started this week."

"I'm not sure," Roger answered, his voice hesitant. "I looked in on your techs from time to time but didn't oversee any new hires. I didn't even know you had any. Why do you ask? Is she not working out?"

"Oh, no, she's working out just fine." Jason smirked to himself as he thought about the beautiful new worker who would be waiting for him bright and early the next morning. "I was just curious." Sensing the doctor was about to ask another question, he feigned a yawn. "I've got to let you go, Roger. These days are still wearing me out."

After saying a quick good-bye, Jason cleaned up his dinner dishes and headed upstairs. A quick shower had him ready for bed before the clock even hit nine PM. He really was tired, as the days seemed far too long to his aching body.

In the bathroom, he took a glance at his pills, then all but sneered at them. *Fuck those pills*, he thought with a grimace. They hadn't done anything for him lately. In fact, they'd made his dreams *worse*. If he was going to heal, it would have to be one hundred percent on his own.

Determined to make it through at least one night of unbroken sleep, Jason downed a beer and crawled into bed, forcing his mind to clear. He was surprised by how exhausted he felt after being so wired all day, but that surprise didn't last long as he was dropped into dreamland.

CHAPTER 9

When he woke in nothing but a pair of sweats, he knew, instinctually, he was still asleep. That fact gave him the courage he needed to step forward into the world he had entered, a harsh world where destruction lurked around every corner of the tiny town with dilapidated dwellings.

Precariously built buildings to his sides toppled over with every step he took. Brick and stone crashed to the ground in rumbles sounding of thunder, as pipe works burst to allow rust-colored water to spew free. Startled, Jason paused, wide eyes taking in the now-fallen town.

Not giving him any time to reflect, the road cracked beneath his feet in tune with the caverns opening up beneath homes before him. From inside those homes residents screamed, their cries abruptly cut off as they fell victim to ruin.

His feet moved before he realized he was even running. A child's cry reached his ears as he approached one of the fallen houses, somewhere behind a pile of splintered wood. Desperately Jason tore at the rubble, the skin around his nails and knuckles tearing with each dig and pull. Finally he saw the smallest hint of skin, then the edges of a shirt. Hope bloomed in Jason's chest. He dug faster, harder...then stopped completely.

A child's chocolate-brown eyes stared up at him, glassy and lifeless. The little boy's body was half buried beneath wooden beams, the top of his head bloody, one arm bent awkwardly at the elbow. With such a tiny frame and no warning to run for protection, the innocent soul had never stood a chance.

Disgust rose in the back of Jason's throat. He didn't need some snake-haired spirit to appear to know this dream was the work of evil. Whatever was wanted from him, they expected to get it by showing him a shattered city resting atop crushed bones. Except, he'd never been a fan of disaster movies depicting thousands dying by explosion and earthquake. Plague and sickness, yes, but that was a different kind of disaster. Biological.

This…this was terrorism at its finest.

"What the hell is this awful place?" he asked, spinning a full circle, trepidation clutching at his heart. Visions of bloody, broken bodies trapped beneath the rubble filled his mind against his will, bringing tears to his eyes. "Jesus Christ. Get me the fuck out of here."

The words seemed to have a life of their own, a statement strong enough to affect the entire world around him. A furious shout echoed across the cloudy sky. He knew, by some power granted to him in sleep he didn't even attempt to understand, the cry belonged to a spirit he was supposed to meet in this dreamland. Perhaps his declaration saved him.

Or brought about my death, he thought when the scene around him began to shift. As though the landscape were made of cloud and fog, it melted away until all that remained was a curtain of absolute nothing.

"Hello?" he called tentatively, not sure which was worse—a place of rubble and destruction, or realm of emptiness.

But then it wasn't empty. Shapes began to form in the fog, slowly at first, then in a blur that left him dizzy. When the world righted itself again, Jason found himself in a place that stank of death and decay.

You seek a different kind of demise, spoke a voice in his head. *I will give you what you desire.*

A river boiled to his right, steam hissing in the early-morning air, bubbles tinted with pink popping over craggy rocks jutting from the surface like broken bones through tender flesh. And in that river floated the dead bodies of silver fish, some of them ripped open to reveal bits of mushy tendon and fat, others glistening beneath a smoldering sun.

The grass was hot and crispy beneath his bare feet, each step creating a new crack in the parched earth. His breath matched the ground—dry, dusty, and tasting of death. But rather than fear gripping his heart as he took in this dying place, Jason was filled with fascination. The land was sick, slowly withering away in its solitude, what evidence of life there might have been now browned, broken, and blowing away in the hot breeze.

He walked farther across this dying desert-forest mix. The sky was gray, ashes drifting down like snow to coat the bare branches of what few trees littered the cratered ground. Each step produced a telling crack, bringing him closer to a pungent aroma that spoke of devastation and decay.

The earth trembled then, forcing Jason to his knees. A split cracked the ground a few feet in front of him, and he watched through wide eyes as a hand protruded from that craggy canyon. Then an arm, and a scarred gray body, until finally a creature he could only describe as terrifyingly grotesque stood before him.

The beast was massive, three legs carrying a bulky body from which three arms protruded. It had no neck, only bouldered shoulders that sloped up to a thick and cracked head with four horns, two pointing behind and two reaching for Jason at the front. Its skin was gray and hard, almost like stone, grating against itself with every small movement, with white eyes scattered across its shoulders and face that contrasted the bleak coloring of its flesh. Jason couldn't decide what was worse, the fact that this creature was completely nude and startlingly human-like in its anatomy, or the stench of sickness wafting off it, a harsh smell of fever and rot.

Jason couldn't speak, so the beast spoke for him.

"Ahh, I do so love when they kneel before me." The voice sounded like rocks over stone, sending a chill down Jason's spine. He watched, still frozen in place, as the beast approached, its nude form grinding and scraping with almost ear-splitting steps. It lowered itself until it was face to face with Jason, eyes roving over the mortal man. Despite his fear, Jason found himself drawn to the creature, wanting to know who it was, what was expected of him, why he had been drawn to this place of death.

When it spoke again, it was through razor-sharp teeth stabbed into bleeding black gums. "You aren't as pretty as the last one."

Jason frowned, wondering what that meant. Were there others? Others for what? Who—

"Tessa?"

"Mmmm," the beast acknowledged as the man finally found his voice, taking a long look at him before straightening and moving back a step. Jason watched the change in its body, the way its eyes closed and stony skin rippled. "A pretty one, she was. So beautiful in her sickness. How I would have devoured her."

Seeing the way the creature responded to the mere memory, *a wild animal in heat*, Jason thought in comparison, he could only imagine what Tessa would have been subjected to had she of been caught by the beast. "How do you know Tessa? Who are you?"

"I am the one they call the Asag," it replied with a sweep of its bouldered arm. "I am the outsider who brings death. I am the sickness that lives in your heart."

Sickness in your heart. The words rang through Jason's mind, too reminiscent of his first dream with the snake-haired woman. "What...what sickness?"

But then he felt it. What started as a dull headache in the center of his forehead built into a throb that pulsed through his entire body. His forehead began to sweat, beads of hot water rolling down his face, down his bare chest and arms. His stomach roiled, and he squeezed his eyes shut as he fought to keep his dinner down. Forcing himself to his feet, Jason intended on running away from the creature, but found himself stuck in place, his body protesting further movement. He was paralyzed, paralyzed as his body began to decay from the inside out.

And yet, he quickly found he didn't want to move after all. The fever was consuming him in small flashes of heat his body welcomed...craved, even. As the burn worked its way through his limbs, Jason felt trickles of pleasure dulling out the pain, warmth spreading to his extremities in a tingling rush. He was all-consumed and he loved it, the way the heat rolled through his veins, the contrast of hot flesh against icy-cold sweat, the carnal hallucinations that began to play out behind his closed eyes. Visions of quivering legs spread before him, the curve of women's bodies pressed against him, full red lips wrapped around his cock.

His concentration was so focused on the feel of pulsing and phantom mouths he didn't notice when the beast moved to stand in front of him. Only when he felt hot breath against his face did Jason open his eyes, drawn into the penetrating stare the Asag had him locked into.

"You embrace the sickness," it rasped, moving so close their bodies touched, one warm and soft and glistening with sweat, the other cold and dry and hard as stone. Jason shivered as the demon moved, sliding around him until it was pressed against his back, until every hard, eager part of the beast's body was pressed against him. "You bask in the glory of death." The rocks-over-rocks voice ground into Jason's ear, seductive in its darkness. He closed his eyes against the voice, not wanting to see what was being done, wanting to experience it all by touch alone.

Cold arms snaked around his waist, sharp nails tracing over the scars that cut across his lower stomach. "Sickness lives within you," the Asag continued, its touch leaving a trail of heat Jason felt pool in his groin. It was wrong, so wrong, he managed to think, but he didn't want the creature to stop. He wanted to be touched, to be desired by the demon.

And so he stood in his fever, listening, waiting.

"I could take away your sickness. Take it away, and put power in its place." The Asag's hands pressed against Jason's gut, and in that move a vision flashed in his mind. Jason, walking without pain or exhaustion. Never going to the doctor again. Exercising in the gym, running on the beach, his body and a woman's joining together in a sweaty tangle of limbs. Jason, running his lab, tending to patients who had fallen ill, so many of them who needed his help. Help he could give, because he was healed. Because he had power.

"Because I will do great things," he whispered.

The vision faded and the demon's hands slid away. Jason opened his eyes to find the Asag once more before him, a grin of cracked tooth and yellow eyes meeting his sight. "Yes," the voice sounded in his mind. "You will be my greatest servant, and you will call me master."

Jason woke from the dream slowly, gently, as though being caressed into consciousness by a lover who shared his bed. He let his body bask in the sensation of warm hands massaging over his arms, down his chest, tender fingers working over the scars that laced his stomach. The longer they massaged, the better the scars felt, like a slow wiping away of pain. A smile crossed his face as he shifted and opened his eyes, disappointed to see the ceiling above him, the bed beneath him, the blankets around him.

It worried him that he wanted to be back in the dream, with the decaying fish and dying earth and creature who called himself the Asag. It wasn't normal to crave the touch of a monster, a male monster, no less. And yet, he wanted to know more about the one who'd called him to dreamland. *Needed* to know more.

Throwing off the blanket, Jason pushed himself from the bed and over to his desk, where he'd set his laptop before going to bed. Once he powered it up, he realized the time, and hesitated. Only about five minutes had passed since he fell asleep, but the dream had felt like hours.

"Weird," he muttered before brushing off the thought and doing an Internet search on the creature. As his fingers played over the keyboard, Jason frowned at the lines of dirt beneath his nails. He used to be so good at keeping up with his appearance, right down to his nails. Such things had slipped his mind lately, in their place worries of getting from the house to the car without collapsing in pain.

"Suck it up," he ordered himself, and returned his focus to the screen. The images that popped up along the top of the page did nothing more than get a laugh out of him—absurd-looking caricatures by people who had clearly never seen the Asag for themselves. But it was the word *demon* scrawled throughout the search results that had his breath stilling and his heart pounding a bit harder than normal.

"Demon?" A flutter of his heart had him pausing, instantly thinking of Tessa. "Mind's playing tricks on you, buddy." And yet, he couldn't stop himself from furthering his research.

Click after click took him to pages on the Asag, stories that told of the beast's penchant for plagues and fever and destruction. Page after page revealed to him the truth of the creature that visited him in sleep, calling to the parts of his soul longing to see the beauty in death. Truth after truth showed him the future he was creating for himself.

A future he could prevent. A future he didn't want to stop.

CHAPTER 10

He got a few more hours' sleep after tiring himself out with seemingly endless research. By the time his alarm went off, Jason was feeling a bit more refreshed, albeit a little perturbed by his nighttime visions. He'd never been the type of person to freak out easily, knowing there was always a rational explanation for everything, always logic in the unexplainable. Whatever was going on with him, there was a medical or environmental cause, and he would eventually get to the bottom of it.

"Just the stress of going back to work," he continued to tell himself as he got ready. "Stress and exhaustion and too much time thinking about Tessa and her fucking murder spree."

He got to the lab a little early, before most of his morning shift would arrive, giving him the chance to take stock of the lab without anyone bothering him now that he was feeling well enough to do so. He did it about once a month, going around to make sure everything was in working order and to see what supplies needed to be ordered. Since he'd been out the past nine months, there was no telling what state the lab was in.

He started with the storage room. Making his way back there, Jason stopped when he saw the dirt that lined the floor in the shape of footprints. Glancing back, he realized they went from the lab door to the storage room and back out. Probably one of the techs who constantly went out for a smoke break before going about his scheduled sticks for the day, since they were on a tight schedule once they got started.

"Great. I work with fucking slobs." Jason sighed and grabbed the broom to clean up the mess. He'd never been a neat freak at home, but he liked his lab spotless. As far as he was concerned, there were enough contaminants around from the hospital patients without having to worry about what the lab workers were bringing in.

Once the mess was cleaned up, he returned to the storage room. Jason took stock quickly, noting the supplies they needed more of. A few more lab coats, for sure, if he could ever get his request for additional staff approved by the administration. There was an unacceptably low supply of syringes, and too few microscope slides. He'd have to remind the staff to keep the supply list updated whenever they took something out.

"Or it's off with your heads for every last one of you," he said to himself, chuckling.

"Something funny, Mr. Waters?"

Startled, Jason spun around, nearly dropping the box of slides he was holding. He wasn't surprised, though, to find Clara standing in the entrance to the storage room wearing a white lab coat, tight black pants, and a form-fitting white shirt. She'd been dressing somewhat provocatively since her first day. Jason had certainly noticed, and while he didn't mind appreciating her beauty, he worried how it would look to others should allow the beautiful new tech to get away with such things.

But she merely continued gazing at him with those gorgeous green eyes, one corner of her mouth tilted up, not at all bothered by whatever favor he was willing to give her.

"Um, nothing," he finally answered, setting down the box. "I was just thinking that I'm going to have to knock some heads together to keep this place running smoothly."

"You're the boss," Clara stated matter-of-factly. Jason found his eyes drawn to her red-painted lips, a couple shades too bright for his taste. For work, he clarified to himself. Any other time, he wouldn't have minded one bit. "You get to take charge. Flex those…verbal muscles."

Frozen in place by those oceans of green, Jason watched as Clara stepped into the storage room, closing the door behind her. Just a few more steps had her right in front of him, and any questions he'd had about whether or not her flirting was intentional were answered when she placed a hand on his arm. "Strong muscles," she said softly, her fingers trailing down his arm, down his hip, across the waistband of his jeans.

"Clara," Jason said in warning, but there was no power in his voice, no real argument. As though she knew he was merely saying her name to show some sort of refusal before finally giving in, Clara only grinned. Her left hand joined the right at the button of his pants and he felt rather than heard the button give way and the zipper slide down.

He knew he should stop her. It wasn't professional, being alone in a dimmed room with a woman he wanted to devour in every way. It wasn't respectable, taking advantage of an innocent new employee who thought she had to make a move on the boss to get ahead in her career. It wasn't right, letting her reach through his open zipper and stroke him with those soft, slender fingers.

But he didn't say a word when she lowered herself to her knees. His hand found the back of her head as she freed him from his jeans, those fingers continuing to stroke his hardened shaft in a mixture of soft and firm squeezes that had his jaw clenching. When those red lips opened, his eyes narrowed in anticipation, and he watched as she took him deep in her mouth, the feel of her warm and wet against him. Her own eyes were closed as she found a steady rhythm. Jason matched that rhythm, gently rocking his hips to push himself deeper still, threading her hair through his fingers and guiding her as she licked and sucked.

Anyone could walk in to find the boss being pleasured by the new girl. Anyone could hear the moans that managed to escape when Clara began a low hum in the back of her throat that echoed against his cock.

No one would stop them in this moment. Jason didn't care who might see or hear. He cared only about the cherry-red lips stretched around his shaft, the delicate hand that mimicked the motions of her mouth at the base, her other hand massaging herself through her pants. His grip on her hair tightened, just as a boiling began low in his belly, a strange mix of rage and desire and possession.

She thought she would own him with her sexual advances. She thought she would gain an upper hand, using her mouth to get ahead in the world. She thought a lot of things that would not work in her favor. But he would let her think them. He would let her pleasure him, foolishly believing all the while she was on control.

Her tongue traced the tip of his cock before she took all of him down her throat, and the single move brought Jason to the edge. He fisted a hand at the back of her head just before he pumped himself into her in a release that had his entire body shuddering. Only when he felt her swallow did he release her and step back to readjust himself.

Clara rose to her feet with that familiar smile, which he now realized wasn't so sweet and innocent after all, but calculating. *Knowing.* She thought she'd gotten one over on him, Jason thought as he watched her wipe at her mouth.

"I hope my job performance is...satisfactory," she said with one brow lifted. There was amusement in her voice, but Jason didn't match the sentiment.

"You think this means something?" he asked, his voice sounding much colder than he'd intended. "Do you think this is a mere joke?"

The smile fell from her face, confusion taking its place. "I...I don't understand. I thought you wanted me."

"I wanted you to corner me in a storage room and suck me off while patients die all around us?"

Indignation filled her eyes. "For someone so concerned about patients, you certainly didn't stop me."

When he saw tears in her eyes, Jason relented, lifting a hand to her cheek tenderly. "Don't cry, Clara," he soothed softly. "You're right. I should have stopped you. I suppose I was caught up in the moment. I'm sorry." He pulled her to him in a gentle hug, and she let him. One arm wrapped around her shoulders while his hand continued to stroke her cheek.

"I'm sorry," he whispered, tightening his hold. "I'm sorry," one more time, before his arm and hand moved against one another, and the resounding *crack* of Clara's neck echoed into his ears.

As her body slumped to the floor, Jason whispered again, "You will never own me." He stared at that beautiful body at his feet, legs twisted, mouth and eyes open in an expression of surprise. She really was pretty, but ignorantly misguided. She thought she would possess him, that mere flirtation-turned-sex would put her on the same level. The sheer foolishness had him laughing.

"I hope my job performance is…satisfactory."

Clara's voice slammed into him, just as the air whooshed out. Jason's head snapped up. There, on this side of the closed storage room door, stood the woman he'd just killed, the woman lying at his feet.

Not at his feet, he realized with a quick glance down. *But… how?* Jason asked himself. Had he dreamed this too? No…He knew his body, and he had just felt the pleasure of a woman's mouth. Hell, his button was still undone. And Clara…she was giving him that stare again, the one that said they shared a secret neither could say aloud.

What was real? He couldn't find an answer, only more questions as his mind struggled to comprehend what was truth and what was a vision his mind cultivated to thoroughly fuck him over.

"I…I have to go." Not looking Clara in the eye, Jason brushed past her and into the lab, where a few of the techs had already arrived and set up their stations.

"Hey, boss. Feeling better?" one of the lab techs asked as soon as Jason walked out of the storage room.

Casting a skeptic glance at the tech, a college intern named Sam, Jason hurried over to his chair. If Sam saw him leaving the room, then surely he saw Clara too, and he wondered if the tech's question was referring to what might be painfully obvious. "What do you mean?"

Sam shrugged. "Figured you must be sick, since you were out yesterday."

The words froze Jason. An icy panic began to crawl over his skin as his mind traced back over the last twenty-four hours. He'd come into work after a particularly memorable dream about Clara, spent the day trying his best not to look at the woman, went home and spoke with Roger about that damned sample again, and went to bed, only to dream about a demon. There were no gaps, no questionable moments, unless he counted the one that just happened in the storage room.

"What do you mean?"

Sam stared at him from the counter, where he was sorting out clean slides into their proper trays. Unwashed black hair fell in his eyes. "Um…I mean…you were out all day yesterday. No one knew why, so we just assumed you weren't feeling well. Did I miss a memo or something?"

"No, no," Jason replied immediately, waving a hand and hoping it looked nonchalant. "I…was just thinking about something else. Sorry, yes. I'm feeling much better."

Except now he was feeling sick to his stomach. If he wasn't in the lab yesterday, then where the hell was he?

*

The question haunted Jason the rest of the day. Though he pretended otherwise, he was thoroughly nauseated by the fact everyone seemed to think he had been out yesterday, and even sicker that he'd envisioned himself killing Clara right after she'd gotten on her knees in front of him. He was almost convinced the blowjob actually happened, judging by how his body felt. But neither of the spoke about it after, and he certainly wouldn't be the one to bring it up.

He left the lab as soon as the night crew arrived, reminding them to keep a regular log of supplies needed and to clean up after themselves should they track in dirt. Then he fled the place that was starting to feel like a grave, or a psych ward; he wasn't sure which. Deciding to stop by the grocery store for a few supplies, he turned right instead of left out of the parking lot and made the quick drive.

The store was close to empty when Jason entered, pulling a cart from the rack and beginning the long trek up and down each aisle. He preferred doing his grocery shopping at night after work, when most people were home eating dinner or getting ready for bed. Crowds annoyed and exhausted him, especially these days.

As he walked up and down the aisles, he found himself leaning heavily on the cart, relying on it far too much. He'd left his cane in the car, knowing he'd have the cart to act as another pair of legs, a stronger pair. Not that he would have used the cane anyway. He despised that stick of wood.

Trying to think through the pain already burning across his stomach, Jason mentally went through his grocery list. Items to make a salad. Twelve-pack of beer. Spaghetti. Maybe some chips and salsa to indulge in a treat every now and then. Roger's birthday was coming up; a card would be thoughtful. In the card aisle, Jason glanced through a few, trying to find one that was more amusing than sentimental.

"Waters?"

Jason closed the card he'd been reading and glanced to his left, a smile blossoming when he saw one of his old college buddies. "Eric! What's up?"

The boy he'd known to be gangly and unfashionable had grown up, filling out into a lean form dressed in trendy jeans and a button-down shirt. His once-unruly blond hair was swept back and perfectly styled. "Not much," Eric answered with a grin. "Haven't seen you since college. Heard you got that job at the hospital you were always talking about. How's it working out for you?"

"Pretty well," Jason answered honestly. All other things in his life aside, he really did love his job. "You? End up working in a pharmacy like you wanted?"

"You know it. So." Eric's eyes swept down briefly before returning to Jason's face. "I heard about the attack. I wanted to stop by the hospital but figured it would be a little weird. Everything okay now?"

Shifting, always uncomfortable talking about himself and the accident, Jason nodded. "It's getting there."

He was saved from having to say anything else by a shout at the end of the aisle. He and Eric watched as two early-twenties women knocked into a display, sending several bottles of shampoo to the floor. They only laughed and continued with their mock wrestling over a cell phone. A young man appeared from around the corner, shouting profanities at them both, then directing his cursing at one of the cashiers who was attempting to quiet them while cleaning up the mess.

When the trio had disappeared to another part of the store, Jason looked back at Eric, who rolled his eyes. "We need a new plague," he said absently, checking his phone for the time.

"Something to get rid of all these morons clogging up the world for the rest of us. Anyway, I've got to run, but we should catch up soon. Hey, are you going to the game this weekend?"

It took Jason a moment to switch gears. His mind was already hooked into a fantasy of the world missing a few billion people, the ones they could all stand to live without. "Um...the football game? No." Then he laughed. "Should I be expecting a big win this time?"

At that, Eric grinned. "Well, I can't argue with that." He clapped a hand on Jason's shoulder, then handed him a business card announcing his title as CFO of a local bank. "Give me a call if you change your mind. I'll be there with the family. We're tailgating with some people from work before the game." He waited until Jason took his card with a nod, then turned and headed in the opposite direction of the rabble-rousers.

Jason stared after him, Eric's words still echoing in his ears. *We need a new plague.* A new plague to wipe away the callous and cold, the irresponsible and obnoxious. A cleansing the world so desperately needed. A fresh start for those who deserved to be rid of the scourge.

We need a new plague.

Oh, how sweet it could be.

CHAPTER 11

The lab was quiet when Jason entered just days after his encounter at the grocery store, days filled with daydreams of a world without the vermin. What little activity there was in the lab went unnoticed, his mind already fogged with possibilities being whispered to him from a voice he did not know, but welcomed all the same.

Go into the storage room, it ordered, an unseen force directing his feet.

Find the box behind the needles, it commanded, reminding him of the secret he'd kept stowed away.

Retrieve the items hidden away, it instructed. *A piece of bark, a chunk of tree root from deep within the earth, a small baggie of dirt, a seedling from a weed growing atop infected soil.*

Remember your purpose, it encouraged, letting Jason forget that second trip he'd taken to Savannah to retrieve those items, making him recall what to do with them.

The virus thrived within Tessa's blood, he knew, but how? Locked in the back room, Jason pulled the year-old blood sample from the cooler and got to work, using a viral culture to identify the virus and begin breaking it apart. But he wasn't finished with just the blood.

Drawing on his many years of study, both collegiate and personal, Jason began extracting samples from the environmental subjects, thin needles carefully slid into the heart of bark, seed, root, soil, to find the abnormalities and harvest them. There was something foreign in Tessa's blood, and whatever it was, it came from these tainted samples.

Tainted, a gravelly voice spoke in his mind, the single word telling him what must be done. Helping him, inspiring him. His hands moved of their own accord, making medical discoveries his brain couldn't even comprehend at this time—a virus hundreds of years old laying dormant in the earth, giving life to the vegetation that grew around it, mixing with the blood of a woman who happened to cut herself on a tree and expose the open wound to the awaiting sickness.

Before him was proof that life, even life causing death, always found a way, and that an illness many thought to be nearly extinct in their country was still thriving. But Jason didn't care about his discovery. He cared only for these samples containing traces of an old virus and how he could mix them with Tessa's blood—Tessa's potentially demonically *tainted* blood—replicating the virus in all five samples and combining them in a petri dish. The media would enhance its growth over time, strengthen it.

Then, he would have his new virus.

Lowering himself so he was eye-level with the petri dish, Jason whispered, "And I shall call you RYF-2. The Resurrected Yellow Fever."

*

It was done. He had created something vile, something with the power to destroy hundreds, maybe even thousands, of lives. And it would be so simple a delivery. A simple prick to the skin, wait for the virus to incubate, and then infect as soon as it went airborne.

Never had Jason felt so alive, so completely powerful. As he entered his home, his body was still shaking with excitement at what he'd accomplished. He had cultivated disease. He had become the wielder of death. Not a force on this earth could touch him, as he now held the power of a god.

Entering his kitchen, Jason pulled a bottle of beer from the fridge and snapped off the top before sliding onto a stool. His blue eyes stared straight ahead, locked on the clock above the stove and watching absently as the minutes passed.

Tick

Blood tainted with an unknown pathogen, a virus isolated and ready to be cultivated, a mutation no one had discovered until now.

Tick

Careful fabrication of a new disease, one strong enough to create a plague able to decimate entire cities, starting with just one.

Tick

The RYF-2 virus, which he'd nicknamed Resurrect Fever, tucked away in its hiding place and away from prying eyes, but ready, waiting, desiring, demanding to be released.

Tock

"What have I done?" Jason whispered, momentarily broken from his thoughts by the worry slicing through his gut. The gravity of his creation began to weigh on him. His head hung in his hands as he asked himself, "Why are you doing this?"

Because they deserve it, came the answer in his mind, the voice he welcomed, and now, feared. Hands tugged at his hair, trying to pull the voice out, but still it spoke, each word sending a wave of dark calmness through Jason.

Because they give nothing to the world, yet expect everything in return. Selfish people. Greedy people.

Because they take everything they have for granted.

"And must be reminded of how easily it can all be taken away," Jason finished for the Asag. He absently scratched at his arm as he stood, staring down at the empty beer bottle. His brow furrowed. "When the hell did I drink this?"

Shrugging it off as just another lapse in time due to his meds, Jason headed upstairs for a rare night of uninterrupted sleep.

*

The man never stood a chance, the Will O'Wisp thought as he wandered the halls of the dark Savannah house. Curiosity led him to the darkness, pride to his own devastation. Oh, Jason's soul was still his own, but not for long.

The Will O'Wisp had thought it once, but the concern came again as night fell upon the old house: Jason Waters was more susceptible to influence than any soul who had ever crossed paths with the demon wielder. Even Tessa had shown resistance, refusing to give in to the demon who called for revenge until she couldn't stand the harrowing memories any longer.

But Jason, he wasn't driven by revenge, by years of pain locked away in a terrified heart. He was driven by something much more basic—ego, and the desire to be known. The man likely didn't even realize what it was that would be his ultimate end.

Even if he did, the Will O'Wisp considered, tucking itself away into the shadows, it didn't matter. It was too late. Jason Waters had heard the demon's whisper, and welcomed it into his heart.

CHAPTER 12

He didn't know how he got here, at the stadium a few hours before the big game, on the outskirts of the tailgaters. It was as though he woke up from an unknown sleep the moment he stepped from his vehicle. Out of a dream and into reality, he pondered as he glanced around at the green-and-black-decorated vehicles and fans. He could smell hot dogs and hamburgers in the air, could see plenty a red cup.

Game day was in full swing.

Not at all bothered by his sudden appearance downtown, Jason wandered away from his vehicle. In one hand the held the cane he usually brought when he expected long periods of time on his feet. He didn't remember grabbing it from the hall closet, where he preferred it remain hidden, but, then again, he didn't remember the drive to the stadium, either. Doing his best not to rely on the cane, he strolled through the throngs of people, enjoying the fresh air, the laughter and banter amongst friends, the signs of life all around him.

It was refreshing in a way to see that the world was normal. After so many days in the hospital recovering from surgery and nights suffering from dream-state terrors, even more hours spent wondering if he was seeing the world the way it was meant to be seen, Jason took comfort in the familiar. Tailgaters playing games of corn hole. Die-hard fans drunkenly arguing with the opposing team's followers. Music pumping across the lot packed tight with vehicles and people. Excitement building the closer it got to kick-off.

But the longer he watched, the farther he walked, the more that happiness turned to disgust.

Ungrateful bastards, Jason thought bitterly, seeing so many people happy with their lives, walking and laughing and living so easily, without pain. They didn't know how perfect their lives were, how much they took for granted, thinking they were invincible as they went about each day as though it wasn't their last.

"We need a new plague," Jason repeated the words spoken by his college friend not so long ago. "Get rid of the filth."

It would be easy, so easy, he told himself as he looked around the crowd that was unworthy of such revelry. They didn't care how precious life was, how quickly it could all be taken away. They cared only for their own selfish pleasures, wasting life to drunken screaming matches at a football game and provocative attire meant only to show off a blatant need for attention. It disgusted him, all of it. The waste and disappointment the world had become, nothing more than the trash these unappreciative sheep so carelessly threw upon the earth. And all in the name of a party they would later forget.

All it would take was one infection, spreading so fast they wouldn't even know what happened. They would go about their lives, dreading spending time with loved ones, complaining through another day of work, and then it would hit. It would start as a headache, maybe a stomachache. Then the fever would come. They would take medicine, stay home in bed for a few days thinking they had the flu. Maybe a few would go to the doctor, but doctors wouldn't know what to test for, and would send them home with a prescription for an illness that didn't exist within the body.

By the time they went to the hospital, it would be too late. The virus would have spread throughout their veins, perhaps to the bodies of their loved ones. And no one would have the cure.

"What is the *matter* with you?" Jason asked himself, shaking his head and stepping off the sidewalk to lean against one of the brick buildings. The thoughts were too much for him. He wasn't this person, no matter the war between his heart and head. "You are *not* a psycho. These people don't deserve this."

But they do, came the voice in his mind. *They take their lives for granted. They deserve to suffer the consequences of their actions.*

"Stop it," he commanded the ghost of evil in his mind. "I am not like you. I don't want this."

You revel in the heat of the fever. You carry the cure for the world's sickness. You know how to bring death to these people.

He did know, could imagine it now, could almost taste the fear and panic that would ensue. "No." Jason pushed himself off the wall and began the long walk back to his car. His limp was more pronounced, having already exerted himself too much earlier. With a sigh he pushed forward, relying on the cane he'd told himself earlier he absolutely would not use. He wasn't too steady with it, as he'd never taken the time to practice, so his gait was slower than those rushing past him in search of friends and celebration.

"Out of the way, gimp," a rough voice ordered as a red-haired man shouldered past, knocking Jason into the wall. He hit the brick hard, cane clattering to the sidewalk.

"Asshole," Jason muttered in response. He thought he'd said it quietly, but the man turned around. His squinted, bloodshot eyes spoke of his inebriation, as did the stagger when he stalked back to Jason.

"The fuck you just say to me?"

In another life, Jason wouldn't have given a single worry to his safety. His odds against a drunk would have been pretty good, given that he kept himself in good health and shape. But now he was, for all intents and purposes, disabled, and this particular drunk man, with arms thick as tree trunks straining against a tight green shirt, likely wouldn't give a damn.

"Not looking for trouble, man," he said in response, hoping to avoid further confrontation. Before he could say anything else, the man shoved him again, this time hard enough to have Jason's head snapping back against the brick. His stomach twisted in pain as he slid to the sidewalk, one hand going to his head and feeling warm blood mixing with his hair.

"That's what I thought, gimp."

Through blurry vision Jason watched his attacker walk away without a second look back, already laughing with his friends.

While everyone else pretends they don't see you.

Looking around, Jason realized the voice was right. No one offered to help; eyes were averted, and the party went on. Rage had his hands clenching into fists as his heart called for vengeance against those who didn't even have the decency to help an injured man.

"Assholes." His teeth grit together as he watched the passersby, the twisted anger embedded deep in his heart igniting when his cane was kicked a foot out of reach, the offending woman barely offering a glance at her feet as she continued her stroll with her three friends in tow.

You are weak. Even women see you as less than. I can make you strong.

"Strong enough to walk like a man," Jason growled. Strong enough to take back control of his life before Tessa destroyed it.

You are in pain. I can take it away.

"I am so fucking tired of the pain." He bit back a wince when his gut churned, the scars feeling like they were pushing against one another in protest.

You are no one. I can make you their hero.

"And they will grovel at my feet," Jason agreed, seeing it all in his mind—everyone who sent him those looks of pity, everyone who told him to take it easy, everyone who walked past him like he was invisible. They would see him. They would fear him. They would plead with him to save them all.

Tell me what you want, Jason Waters.

And then he didn't care about the consequences anymore. He didn't care what might happen because of his sick obsession. He

certainly didn't care what anyone else would think. He only wanted
the pain to go away, to be the hero in a war he would create, to—
"Make them grovel at my feet."
And, with his command, Jason gave himself over to the Asag.

*

Later, when it was too late to matter, no one would remember
the disabled man who suddenly rose to his feet with renewed vigor.
They wouldn't remember seeing his expression settle into one of
dark intent, or the way his gaze settled on the crowd without really
seeing anyone.

Nor would they remember the attractive man, dressed in a
Jacksonville jersey, strolling through the throngs of tailgaters with
his arms at his sides and hands in fists, staring straight ahead, never
looking back at the destruction he left behind him, destruction that
wouldn't be seen until three to seven days later.

Some of them would remember little pricks of pain in their
arms or legs that momentarily jolted them out of their reverie,
but they would blame the Florida mosquitos or their own drunken
states of mind. And they would forget the figure that had passed
by so calmly at the very moment of their pain.

*

From its prison, the Will O'Wisp watched as Jason gave his
soul over to the one called the Asag. It had been so easy, waiting for
the perfect moment to cast its influence over the unsuspecting soul.
The demon took advantage of the man's weakness—exploited it,
even—until Jason was so ashamed by his helplessness he turned to
the evil promising him greatness.

But greatness, as did everything that seemed to come at so
convenient a time, came with a price. Jason had yet to discover just

how much he would have to pay. For Tessa, the price had been more than her freedom, more than her soul—it had cost Tessa her brother's soul, as well.

The Will O'Wisp thought from the beginning Jason was stronger, but he was also weak. A man driven by ego could easily be brought to his knees. But it wasn't going to watch, had no interest in seeing the takeover and the destruction that came with it. No, it would wait to witness the aftermath, just as it waited for the next victim to enter its lair.

CHAPTER 13

Time escaped him.

Hours between night and day had begun to blur, the time between game day and home and whatever came next, unclear. Jason wasn't sure what day it was when he found himself opening the door to his house. It was dark out, the crickets singing their nightly song, the air just chilly enough to tell him it was later than he probably thought. He didn't remember going to work that day, or where he'd been or what he'd done at all, though he wasn't bothered by the lapses in memory.

In fact, he was perfectly willing to tell himself, "You just need a nice, long nap. And maybe a cold beer beforehand."

Entering the house, Jason dropped his cane by the door and trudged into the kitchen. He may not have known the day or time, but he was fucking hungry. He moved in a blur of motions, barely focusing as he shoved pieces of turkey in his mouth directly from the container and washed it down with a glass of water, then all but attacked a bag of cut broccoli. Only when the rumbling in his stomach finally faded did he take a minute to breathe.

It was then he noticed how hot he was. A fever, he guessed, perhaps accounting for his foggy brain. His doctor had warned him about working too hard his first few weeks back, claiming his body would still be weak and needed to regain the strength to operate at full capacity. Except this didn't feel like exhaustion. It seemed more like a fever and possibly the flu. His skin felt weird also, a strange combination of itchy and smooth.

Absently scratching at his arms, Jason tossed a few stray dishes into the sink, cursing under his breath when the itching only intensified. His scratching intensified, until he was leaving dark red marks in his skin as his nails dug deeper.

"Feeling okay, boss?"

Jason spun around, his back hitting the counter. "Shit, Clara. How...how did you get in here?" he asked, one hand lifting to point at the rather stealthy and potentially stalkerish woman. She'd managed to sneak up on him, and he wasn't sure how, considering the heels she wore showing off those long, toned legs.

She didn't answer him, only closed the distance between them. Finding himself watching her legs and breasts rather than her eyes, Jason forced himself to look up and prepared to ask her to leave with claims it wasn't professional. His protest died on his tongue when she ran her fingers down his arms, and he felt cool relief everywhere she touched. Suddenly he didn't care why she was there or how she'd gotten in. All that mattered was she keep touching him.

"You've dreamed about me," she whispered through those pouty red lips. Her eyes looked up though long lashes.

Swallowing hard, Jason replied, "Yes...more than once."

Her hands traced up his forearms, across his shoulders. "I dreamed about you too, for so long. Do you want to know why?" A brief wait until he nodded, and she smiled. "I've been waiting for you, Jason Waters, for many, many years. Just you, the only one who could free me."

Despite the hesitation creeping into the lust, Jason kept the flirtation going. "Well, good thing you found me."

"Mmm. Good thing indeed." Her hands stopped their roaming, just as his found her hips. "Do you know why it itches, and why I can make it all go away? Your skin," she clarified when he frowned.

Jason stepped back. "How did you know about that?" He

attempted to put distance between them, but Clara closed it just as quickly as he opened it.

"You gave up control," she continued, a sweet smile contradicting her ominous words. "You wished to be strong again, and forsook your soul, and now you feel the consequences."

"The…the consequences? What are you talking about? Who are you?"

"I am the manifestation of darkness. I am the illusion that draws you in. I am the desire that lurks within you."

Silence loomed around them as Jason took in her reply. The recent past came rushing back to him—the dreams dominated by lust, the hallucinations of taking and possessing Clara only to kill her, the way no one else really seemed to know or even acknowledge her around the lab.

Had he really been so blind? Sam never mentioned seeing him come out of the storage room with Clara in tow. Even Roger had admitted he didn't know any new techs were hired.

Before he could voice his concerns, Clara spoke again. "It will pass, that cold, tingling feeling. I just have to get settled in."

"…What? What are you talking about? Who are you?"

"The Asag, of course. Weren't you paying attention?" She smiled at him as though he were a child being taught a lesson in school. "I will settle over you, our flesh joining as one. Together, we will rule this world."

No, he thought frantically, his heart beating and skin burning, he'd seen the Asag. It was a grotesque beast with stony skin and eyes all over its shoulders and face. Not this beautiful creature before him, the one he'd dreamed about, the one who'd been on her knees to service him.

I am the illusion, she'd just said. *The manifestation of darkness.*

Could the Asag change forms? Could the demon manifest itself into a form Jason would desire, could be lured in by?

The bones beneath Clara's skin began to ripple. Jason found

himself reaching out, fascinated by the transformation. "What... what's happening?"

Clara smiled a grotesque grin that stretched too large across her face. "Now, you see the truth."

She showed him that truth in a flash of power that sent him flying back against the countertop. A face that contorted into something boney and sharp and gray. Green eyes that sunk back into gaping sockets. Gorgeous curves stretching into a body too distorted and large to house human bone and muscle.

"The Asag," Jason whispered, eyes wide at the sight of this half-woman, half-demon monster.

"You will call me master," she rasped, her voice like grating rocks, like the Asag who visited him in dream.

Torn between being terrified by this beast and furious at the attempt to be owned, Jason stood rooted in place. He couldn't think, couldn't make sense of the scene of complete insanity in his kitchen. Though, one fact was clear as day.

"I will never call you master."

He expected her to rage, or fight, or argue, and was shocked when she began to laugh. It was a bitter sound, telling him she didn't believe his claim. Then in a simple shimmer of air she was gone, and Jason was left alone in his too-bright kitchen, staring at the spot a beautiful woman once stood and wondering if he'd finally reached the moment of his psychotic break.

Was this how Tessa had felt when her mind began to go? Was it all because of the Savannah house, some kind of psychosomatic effect making him see things? Or, worse, was he really going crazy, and would soon turn into another Tessa and Braden Taylor? His breath shuddered out of him. One hand gripped the counter as he forced his feet to move, desperately needing to get the hell out of the kitchen.

"Distraction. You just need a distraction," Jason told himself, walking into the living room and fumbling around in the dark for the remote. The thought of turning on a light terrified him, lest any more women-turned-demons were interested in making an appearance.

The TV blazed to life and he settled down on the couch without bothering to change the channel. Head hung in his hands, Jason listened half-heartedly to the news report. Something about a stolen car, another about a local bakery celebrating its fiftieth anniversary in the area. The weather report at the top of the hour signified the slow change of the seasons, or as close to seasons as Florida got, anyway.

"Just normal people in a normal world," he mumbled.

But then the news anchor said something that wasn't so normal after all. "And continuing the spree of killings across the United States, the Taylor Sibling Slaughters has another murder added to its numbers. Forty-year-old Annie Everly of southern Florida was found by her nine-year-old daughter in the bathroom of their Miami home, decapitated and with a wound to her lower stomach."

Jason looked up, staring at the television through his fingers in horror as the news anchor continued. "Everly's daughter called the police after hearing her mother scream, and seeing two figures walk out the front door. She later confessed to her late mother's physical and sexual abuse. The child is now in the custody of her father, who divorced Everly three years ago and was not aware of his ex-wife's abuse."

The screen changed to a picture of the house, roped off by police tape. It was just a normal single-story house with nothing foreboding about it. But as another reporter appeared on the screen, what lay beyond those normal walls was enough to have his stomach churning. She gave enough details on the murder and victim to paint a picture of what the Taylor siblings had done, and what they'd done with the entrails.

"Jesus Christ, Tessa."

"Christ wants no part of Tessa Taylor," said a voice to his right, nearly sending Jason to the floor as he jumped and scrambled to his feet. He tripped over the coffee table, cursing himself as he fell against the wall and flicked on the lamp. The room was awash in a soft yellow glow, and there was a woman, her short blonde hair framing her face in soft curls, her curvy body perched on the armrest of a recliner tucked in the corner of the room. Sitting in the chair was a tall and lanky man with black eyes that matched his hair.

"Who the hell are you?!" Jason barked, one hand curling around the base of the lamp. In his panic he didn't realize there was something familiar about her, but it wouldn't take long for recognition to set in.

His eyes widened when the two intruders only smiled, and he blinked when they began to change...entire bodies altering right in front of him so delicately he wasn't sure if he was imagining the transformation or if they'd ever looked a certain way to begin with. It was as though a veil lifted, softly and subtly transforming the strangers into familiar faces. Blonde hair turned black, curves melted into a short, thin frame. "What the..."

"Tessa," Jason breathed when the illusion floated away completely, not sure if he should be afraid, furious, or happy to see her. He stared across the room. One part of him wanted to flee, the other was curious why she was there. "How...?"

The woman he once knew as Tessa Taylor pushed herself off the chair, strolling across the room and stopping halfway as though expecting him to meet her. For some reason, he did, pausing a few feet away. "I'm sorry for the illusion," she said, the sound of her voice not like he remembered. "It's the only way we can travel and continue our cause. Only when traveling, though. When we take their lives, it's just Tessa and Braden again. We like our victims to see our real faces."

Right now, her real face terrified him more than the illusion. He couldn't even fathom about how she was able to make herself look like someone else, let alone think about what she looked like to her victims when their blood was coating her hands. "What... what are you doing here?"

"You understand now," she replied. "You understand what happened. Savannah. The house, the bid."

More questions than answered flooded his mind. "What? The supposedly haunted house? What bid? What are you talking about?"

A frown crossed her pretty face, still so delicate-looking despite the horrors it had seen and done. "The Will O'Wisp didn't tell you?"

"The what? What the fuck is a Will O'Wisp?" Jason glanced from Tessa to Braden, who was still sitting in the shadows, watching them both. The younger Taylor had always been quiet, but Jason was unnerved by his silence now. Turning his eyes back to the woman before him, he jerked reflexively when she lifted her hands to his face.

"Relax, Jason. I'm going to show you the truth. I'm not going to hurt you."

"Not going to hurt me?" he repeated incredulously. "Have you forgotten slicing me to shreds in the hospital? You almost killed me, you psychopath! And if you're not here to finish the job, then what the fuck do you want? Round two?"

His rant left him breathless, and he stepped back to put distance between himself and his would-be murderer. But Tessa only offered a small smile and looked at him the way she used to— like he was someone she greatly admired, and she wanted to know everything he did about the world.

"Don't do that."

Her smile only deepened. "Don't do what?"

"Don't look at me like nothing has happened." Jason threw an arm in the TV's direction. "Tessa, you almost killed me, and I still have no idea why. Now you and your brother are off murdering people. Jesus Christ," he said again, hands tugging at his hair. "I can't deal with this. I just watched a woman I thought was a new lab tech turn into a fucking demon in my kitchen, then disappear into thin air. Now you're appearing after she disappeared, and you don't look like you, and then you do. And your brother's over there, staring at us like he's waiting for something to happen. Maybe cut me open again like you did the first time. How the hell do you even get away with it? How have you become this nationwide murderer and not get caught?"

Tessa sank to the couch, cocking her head to the side in a silent invitation for him to do the same. Realizing she wasn't going to talk until he sat, he did, putting as much distance between them as he could.

"So many questions," she said quietly. "To be perfectly honest, I never wanted to kill you, Jason. I only wanted you out of the way. You were standing between me and my freedom. I am sorry for what you've gone through," she admitted, casting her eyes down at his shirt-covered abdomen and imagining what scars must be hidden beneath. "You never meant any harm. You didn't deserve to suffer."

"Well, gee, that means so much," he quipped, crossing his arms. "I'm so glad you never meant to kill, only cause me nearly a year of surgeries and physical rehab and a lifetime of pain."

"A lifetime?" It was both a question and a knowing smirk that he didn't yet understand. "And we don't murder *people*, Jason. We exact revenge on those who have forsaken their duties as loving caregivers. They are not people. They are beasts, less than man, less than animal."

A laugh escaped before he could stop it. Jason ran his hands through his hair, bewildered by the conversation taking place in his living room. "Exacting revenge? Less than man and animal? Tessa, you don't talk like that. What is going on?"

Tessa smiled again. "You already know," she replied, one arm sliding along the back of the couch, her fingers dangerously close to his shoulder. "You let him in. You gave him control over your soul. Even now you feel him within you. You hear his whispers. You sense his power."

"Sense who? Hear who?" When she didn't respond, only cocking her head to the side curiously, Jason took a moment to reflect. He'd been so concerned with the she-devil once named Clara that he hadn't had a moment of silence to determine how he was feeling. Now, he realized he did hear something in the back of his mind, a whispering he couldn't quite make out, as though someone were playing a radio softly in the background. His flesh, which had begun to itch earlier, had settled down but still felt like it was covered by a kind of thin, skin-tight material. And, the more he thought about it, the more uncomfortable it all became.

"What the hell is happening to me? You know, don't you?"

Tessa's fingers danced lightly on the couch as she observed him. One tap, two, three, a silent song playing out to her words. "You're stronger than she was. Even as he settles over you, still your mind is your own. Perhaps you two will co-exist."

Jason was watching her hand with black-painted nails, wondering if he was about to be ripped open again, so it took a moment for her words to register. "She?" he repeated, finally lifting his eyes to hers. Not Tessa's eyes, he realized with a sinking sensation in his stomach. Oh, they looked the same in color and shape, but there was something dark about them, a stare that was too penetrating. "What do you mean, *she?*"

Tessa lifted a shoulder, then tapped her temple with one finger. "I still hear her sometimes, back here. She screamed a lot, at first, gave me an awful headache. Begged me to let her go, to let her brother go. I had to show her a better way, everything we could do together now that we are bonded. And now, she laughs. Each time we take the head of another beast, she laughs, and I laugh with her."

Jason was silent for a moment, digesting what he was being

told. It was absurd…wasn't it? Tessa claiming not to be herself, but instead…what? Locked away in her own mind, driven insane by what he could only guess was some sort of evil spirit or demon. Or was she insane, and the woman before him was still Tessa, just some twisted, schizophrenic version of herself? Did she actually enjoy the murders? Could he really believe the woman in front of him wasn't really Tessa? And if it wasn't Tessa, then who was it?

He couldn't ask himself any more questions. The stream of consciousness was driving him crazy all on its own, so he decided to ask her one instead.

"Are you saying I'm not talking to Tessa, but to a…a demon?"

"Demon is such a misguided word." Tessa smoothed back her black hair and lifted her chin with a grimace. "I have a name. Had a name, once. Now I go by Tessa Taylor. But even with my beautiful new host, why must every spirit without flowing white wings be labeled as something so vile and evil?"

"And what about him?" Jason nodded toward Braden, who was now looking out the window. "If you're seriously claiming to be…possessing?…Tessa, then how does he play into this?"

Tessa glanced over her shoulder. Her face softened into an expression so loving that Jason could have sworn she truly was a big sister looking after her baby brother. "Braden became something dark and destructive many years ago. His mother made him what he is, and his father allowed it to happen. He fooled the authorities into believing he had overcome his past, but it was always there, right at the surface, just waiting for the opportunity to be freed. I help him hone his rage into a more…effective outlet. He was more than happy to succumb to my influence and join his sister. Now, they will always have each other. Tessa and Braden against the world. Their souls will always be united."

She tapped her temple again, and Jason wasn't sure what she meant but was too confused to even ask. Only one thought could focus in his mind. "I want to talk to Tessa." He thought she…*it*…

would argue, but instead she said nothing, only staring at him with a smile until he saw the subtle shift in her eyes as though a cloud had floated away in the breeze. "Tessa?"

The young woman smiled, the grin so bright and familiar he knew she—the real Tessa—was back, even if only momentarily. "Jason!" She reached out to hug him, then pressed her lips together when he recoiled. "Right...Jason, I'm so sorry for what I did. I wasn't...well, I wasn't in my right mind." A chuckle escaped and she shook her head.

He didn't match her amusement. "Tessa, what's going on? How did you let this happen?"

"I didn't *let* anything happen. Well, not at first anyway." Her expression turned somber. "The Pontianak, she followed me home from Savannah. At first I was afraid. She made me remember all the awful things from my past, made me feel like I did when I was a little girl. I didn't want to remember those things, but she showed me anyway. I never would let that happen."

A shudder worked its way through her thin shoulders. "She made me remember all the hate and resentment I'd kept locked up for so many years. Then I realized something amazing. She was right, Jason. I *did* want revenge. I just never had the courage or ability to take it before I met her. So then, yes, I let her in, so I could have my revenge."

"So you killed your parents, and recruited your brother, all for revenge."

"Not just for revenge," Tessa clarified. "For *freedom*. Freedom from nightmares, from being afraid of the dark like I was still some kid crying in the corner. I'm free from the restraints of the world. I can go wherever I want, be whoever I want to be, and kill the people who don't deserve to walk the world with us. And Braden," gentle eyes met her brother's, both of them smiling, "now it's him and me, just like it always was and always will be."

Completely nuts, he decided, except he wasn't sure if her insanity was genuine or self-imposed. "Tessa, is this really what you want?"

One hand traced patterns on the couch cushion as she replied, "I'm free, Jason." Her voice was soft, sad almost. "I don't have nightmares anymore. I'm not afraid of the dark. Braden and I, we can laugh and joke again. We aren't afraid."

"But you're killing people."

"People who *deserve* it. People who mistreat their children, some of them so horrible you can't even imagine what these little boys and girls go through." She sighed when Jason only shook his head, knowing they would never agree. So, she changed the subject. "Have you heard from Ben?"

Jason's eyes narrowed at the mention of her fiancé. Or, rather, *ex*-fiancé, he considered. He wasn't sure why, but the name sent a spike of jealousy through him. "I haven't talked to him since you... well, you know. I heard he moved away, or was planning on moving."

"Good for him. I hope he can start over and find someone who can love him with all her heart. He deserves it." Tessa nodded, taking in a deep breath. Jason could see the regret spread across her face for the only man she'd ever loved. When he didn't say anything, she smiled again. "You wanted to talk to me, Jason. So, talk."

He did want to talk, but this was weird. She was too happy, to chipper talking about things that should have made her sad or even disgusted, and the old Tessa was never this happy. The old Tessa, the *real* Tessa, was spunky and sarcastic. Still, this person next to him was the best chance he had at explaining things. "Okay, well. First things first, I guess. Why are you here?"

With a shrug, Tessa settled back against the couch. "We were down south making our way back north, and I figured we'd stop by and see how you were doing, and clean house while we were here. We haven't been back to Florida since I left. And...she sensed that another soul had been taken by one of the spirits she'd been trapped with, and wanted to see what had become of you."

"...She?"

"Yes, she." There was that eerie smile again, happy when she should have been frightened. "The one who freed me. She is a friend, Jason. She won't harm you, or the one who now holds your soul."

The Asag. He remembered the beast from his dreams, the one Clara had claimed now took hold of his body. That rock-and-slate body, the horns, the perversion at seeing his feverish body. "Do you know what's happening to me?"

"Yes."

"...Are you going to tell me?"

"It would be easier to show you."

"How are you going to—" Jason froze when Tessa shifted suddenly and straddled him. A momentary flash of panic struck him before she settled down on his lap, her hands gripping his shoulders, and it became clear she had no intention of harming him. "What, um, what are you doing?"

Tessa lifted a brow. "Don't tell me you never thought about this, boss."

Jason became acutely aware of her legs on either side of his hips, her slender fingers in his hair, his body's immediate throbbing response to the lust that surrounded them both. He'd always thought she was pretty, beautiful even, but she'd been off-limits. Both as an employee and a fiancée to another man. And, yes, there had been a dream or two that he'd used as inspiration for his more...carnal...fantasies. But he respected boundaries. Now she was offering herself to him, but was it really her?

He didn't care, he decided. They were in this together, whatever *this* was, and so he grinned a feral grin that had a growl forming low in her throat. "Let me show you," she whispered, only a second before their mouths came crashing together.

CHAPTER 14

Jason wrapped an arm around Tessa's back, yanking her closer. Her tongue swept past his lips and he enjoyed her sweet taste. The innocence he'd always associated her with was gone, replaced with something erotic and fierce, and he was more than willing to take everything she was willing to give.

But then she pulled back, breaking their kiss with such force his mind spun. Before he could ask what was wrong, he realized the answer.

"Shit," he cursed, nearly throwing Tessa off his lap when he saw that they were no longer in his house, but sitting on a log somewhere deep in the woods. Perhaps sensing his fear, Tessa moved off him and stepped over to her brother, who had apparently come into the vision with them and was sitting on a log opposite the duo.

Ignoring them both, Jason took in his surroundings. Towering trees that canopied them against the sky and stars. Thick underbrush that twisted and coiled, barely restraining at the edges of a narrow path. A small clearing where he stood with four logs surrounding a well-used but currently burned-out fire pit. The only light came from what little moonlight filtered through the trees.

Not the only light, came a voice in his mind, and Jason found his head turning to see an orange glow in the distance. It came closer, until the glow was a bright light the size of a basketball. His eyes narrowed as he tried to make out the shadowed figure behind the strange floating orb.

The Will O'Wisp. The name was said with both veneration and condemnation by a voice that sounded like rocks tumbling over one another.

Jason didn't notice Tessa and Braden step back into the shadows. His attention was focused on the figure with light for hands, desperately trying to figure out what it was, what it meant. Taking a step closer, Jason watched as the one Tessa and his mind's voice called the Will O'Wisp edged its way closer, only to turn away when something to its left caught its attention. Jason followed the creature's gaze to see a woman stumbling in the dark.

Feet rooted in place, Jason watched the ball of light float closer to the woman, who was dirty and close to hysterics. Her skin was smudged with mud, face stained with tears, hair in disarray from rogue branches. And she was barefoot, her feet bloody from the wayward trail. Her teary eyes widened when she saw the light, but before she could scream, it spoke.

"You are lost on the path," it said with a voice seeming deceptively calm. "You flee from terror, and in your flight, have lost your way."

The woman looked from the light to the forest to the shadowed figure. Her fear was evident on her face, but there was something else, a hint of determination to be brave, as well. "Help me," she asked. "Please show me the way home."

Jason wondered why she was so eager to take help from what he could only describe as another demon, but the creature didn't seem bothered by her easy acceptance. "Come with me," it said, holding out the hand not covered in glowing light. "I will take you out of this wretched forest."

It took the woman by the hand, but instead of leading her along the narrow path, it began to drag her into the woodland. She protested with a cry, attempting to yank her arm free. But the Will O'Wisp held tight, all but dragging her into the trees, closer to where Jason stood. Neither took notice of him as they passed, one struggling against an iron grip, the other pretending not to hear her pleas.

"Struggling is in vain," it told her, with not a care in its voice. "I once struggled against the task I was given, to help the wayward traveler. And in my struggle I was trapped to this cursed place, forced to forever haunt this forest that was once my beautiful home, now nothing more than a prison."

The Will O'Wisp stopped, and for once Jason could clearly see its nude form. It was lanky, spindly even, with long legs and awkwardly high hips, coarse brown fur covering nearly every inch of skin, and a tail. Its face was comical, with oversized features and two horns protruding from mangy black hair.

"And now, as do all who struggle, you too will find the prison meant for you."

Jason expected the woman to start crying again, and was surprised when she laughed. A true, genuine laugh, which startled the Will O'Wisp enough that he dropped her arm. "You once were a great helper of man," the woman said, all traces of fear gone from a voice strengthened by conviction. "Now you seek to destroy, to lead astray those who are already lost."

She began to circle the Will O'Wisp, lake-blue eyes turning dark as her light-colored hair whipped around her sharp face in a sudden breeze. "You say this is your prison. You say all those who struggle must pay, as though you are the almighty, the ever-powerful granted with the gift, nay, the *right*, to cast just judgment."

The woman regarded the Will O'Wisp with an air of judgment all her own. "Perhaps it is time you become what you already desire to be."

The lights dimmed as the creature hesitated. It seemed to see something in the woman's gaze, hear something in her words, that Jason couldn't comprehend. Just as quickly as it moved to take the woman to places unknown, it became humbled. "Madam, I didn't realize you were—"

"His greatest servant?" she finished for him.

"This was a test?"

She lifted a brow. Her gaze held no warmth for what the Will O'Wisp's future held. "A most important test," she answered. "He has been watching you, Will O'Wisp, seeker of the lost man. And he sees great potential in you."

"To do what?" the creature asked hesitantly, half-turned as though poised to flee at a moment's notice. "How can I be of service to the great master?"

At the question, the woman smiled. It was a cold, calculating smile, one that chilled Jason down to his toes. She crept closer to the Will O'Wisp, who was now still as a statue. "He has a task for you, one that will free you of this wretched forest forever."

Form his place at the edge of the clearing, Jason frowned, starting to put the pieces together. Tessa had spoken of the Will O'Wisp, who he now realized was the holder of the flickering flames he'd seen in the house in Savannah. A creature that once helped lost travelers, becoming twisted, turned into something dark by a servant of the great master.

Satan? Jason wondered, rolling his eyes at himself. He wanted to ask how the Will O'Wisp's light transformed into some kind of carrier for the demons he saw in his sleep, how it came to haunt the Savannah home, why it allowed itself to harbor such evil and inflict such pain on innocent people. He wanted to know how it went from helping the lost and scared to a beacon that sent a honing signal straight down to Hell. But just as he opened his mouth to speak, he saw that he'd waited too long, and that he was alone in the forest.

"Hello?" Jason called, taking a step into the clearing. Only the sound of crickets at his back crackled in response. "Um…Tessa? Will…O…Wisp?" Even the name sounded idiotic. "Tessa? *Tessa!*"

Jason jolted upright, the sound of his own shout erupting him from the dream-vision. It took his eyes a second to adjust to the bright light of his living room and the feel of his couch beneath him. Leaping off the couch, he peered around, expecting to see his two surprise visitors, but they were nowhere to be found.

Jason was alone, with only the taste of Tessa's kiss to remind him that he wasn't going completely insane.

*

As Jason dreamed of the one who led him to ruin, just eight blocks over, another was beginning to experience his own.

The man, a burly brute with fiery-red hair, sat on the side of the bed with his head in his hands. A cough ruptured through him, tearing at his chest, a garbled sigh mingling with the phlegm in his throat. It felt like a fire poker was being jabbed behind his eyes.

"Keven?" a quiet, timid voice asked behind him. "Are you okay?"

"Do I sound okay?" he snapped at his girlfriend, who bit down on her bottom lip with downcast eyes. The man named Keven rose from the bed, muttering, "Fucking idiot," as he stomped to the bathroom and slammed the door shut. There, he braced himself against the sink, fighting back another round of coughs while pawing through the cabinet above the sink for anything close to medication.

Eying a few leftover bottles of painkillers from his girlfriend's surgery a few months ago, Keven snapped off the tops and downed a small handful, washing it down with water from the tap. He didn't care what he took so long as it knocked him out enough to avoid this shitty cough. He wouldn't look weak, refused to, especially in front of someone as useless as the one in his bed.

The rattling cough seized him again, causing him to hunch over the sink with an arm lifted to cover his face—except this time, when he pulled his hand away from his mouth, his fingers were painted red. "What the fuck," he said, his voice cracking at the sight of thick blood clotted over his skin.

"Keven?"

"Shut the fuck up!" he shouted in response to the woman in the other room, spitting a mouthful of blood into the sink. He heard her sigh and was about to yell at her to get the fuck out of his bed and house before he beat the shit out of her when he noticed the blood dripping from his nose.

"Are you fucking kidding me?" Grabbing a handful of toilet paper, he wiped at the blood, wincing when the headache intensified to a pulsing hammer in the center of his forehead. Heat flashed through him, the beginnings of a nasty fever, just as his vision blurred against the agony behind his eyes. For a moment he could only see blurs of red in the mirror.

"What the fuck," he said again, this time quieter so the nag in his bedroom wouldn't start chattering again. He was never sick. He worked hard to make sure of it. Five days a week in the gym, protein shakes, staying away from the dipshits at work who sneezed all over the place. *Sick* wasn't acceptable to him, and he looked down on anyone who ever complained of being ill.

But this didn't feel like a regular cold, or even the flu he normally heard people bitching about. No, he felt...wrong, he realized. Like something inside him was breaking and spilling out in his guts. And just as that realization hit, so too did the slice in his stomach like teeth clamping down on his intestines. He dropped to the toilet with a grunt, his bowels releasing in a burning stream that had sweat dripping down his thick biceps and a chill racing up his spine.

Helpless to do anything but wait for what felt like his entire body to empty, Keven pushed back his sweat-dampened hair with one hand and held a hand towel to his nose with the other. The headache continued to pound, but in this moment he was relieved he wasn't sick from both ends.

A bitter copper stench met his nostrils through the towel, much stronger than the small trail leaking through his nose was capable of producing. His brow furrowed as the breath heaved out of him. All around the smell thickened, a foreboding prequel to what he knew would be a nasty flu. Though he didn't want to, he dared a look into the toilet, eyes widening when he saw the bowl was filled with blood.

He started to call out to his girlfriend, finally able to admit defeat just this once, but his vision began to fade, along with his consciousness. Before he could attempt to clean himself, he slumped to the floor in a pile of his own blood and filth.

*

It knew what Jason saw in the vision Tessa gifted him, as it watched in its mind's eye the revelations of the past. The beginning of its imprisonment, the trickery that began as a promise and ended with the lie trapping him in a lifetime of servitude to its greatest master. Imprisonment had been its own fault, but such a fact didn't take away the sting of being caught.

Jason wasn't shown everything—how the spirits came to replace the light the Will O'Wisp once held so dear, how it moved from place to place over the centuries and eventually came to rest in this dark and ominous house, how it was able to see the pain it caused by allowing itself to turn into something dark and evil. Perhaps that was a story for another time.

It was for the best, the Will O'Wisp considered, tucking itself into the shadows to await its next victim. Few knew the entire story, and those who did often never regained control of their souls to tell anyone. Not that it mattered, as no one would ever believe the ravings of madmen who claimed to be caught by the demon. And Jason was already lost to the spirit that had made its claim, even if he didn't know it yet.

Jason didn't seem to care he only knew part of the story or that his guests had vanished. Upon waking to find himself alone, he merely shook his head and retired to his bedroom with memories of a kiss on his lips. He slept soundly that night, unaware that his first victim would soon be revealed. And so the Will O'Wisp sighed, knowing its time with the demon of sickness had come to an end, but now unable to look away from the devastation it would create.

CHAPTER 15

Indeed, Jason still thought he held control over his own self as he arose the next morning feeling surprisingly refreshed and energized for the day ahead. His sleep had been filled with memories of what he was now convinced was a hallucination. Clara showing up in his lab at the most convenient of times, Tessa and Braden appearing in his living room, Tessa's attempt to seduce him, a ghastly-looking figure being tempted by a not-so-lost woman in the woods. And, perhaps worst of all, that the murderer-turned-seductress was claiming he was possessed by a demon who somehow latched on to him from the Savannah house.

But trying to process that information made him feel like he was going insane, and so he chose not to acknowledge it at all, labeling it as a hallucination brought on by stress, and maybe those pills he'd been prescribed. It was easier to pretend, for now, that the stress of returning to work was messing with his head.

If he really thought about it, he would have wondered why it was so easy to disregard the unexplainable things happening to him. But, if he *really* thought about it, he'd also realize that something was preventing him from thinking at all. Which was why Jason walked into the lab with hardly a thought to his vision of the Will O'Wisp, and nary a memory of the past week save for the ones he was permitted to remember.

Jason entered the hospital, immediately stopping when he saw the bustle of activity. This early, there were rarely more than a few nurses making the rounds; now the hall was a flurry of activity.

Doctors shouting at one another, gurneys being pushed down halls. Too much was happening at once to make sense.

But it wasn't the activity that made him hesitate. No, it was the masks that had his feet stuck to the cold tile floor.

Gruesome leather beaks protruded from the faces of nurses and doctors, eyes peering through scratched glass circles, wide weather-worn straps wrapping around the backs of their heads to hold the masks in place. Each beak stretched and curved, sharp and scarred peaks accentuated by the shadows behind the glass oculars. Long white coats clinging to ankles swept down from their collars, making it appear as though the figures floated on air as they rushed to the elevators or into patients' rooms. As Jason watched, they began to slow, his vision tunneling into a blur that focused only on the figures directly in front of him.

Days of old become anew, came a voice echoing all around him. A rough, hard voice like grating stone. *See the sickness of the past. See what I have brought you.*

He began to move through the crowd, the scent of lavender and roses trailing behind him as the masked figures parted for his passing. Heads turned slowly, glassy obscured eyes watching him without really seeing, long beaks reaching toward him in warning of the death just beyond each door.

His breath caught in his throat when the walls began to undulate in a blur of gray. The ground beneath him shivered and flashes of black smoke curling toward a dark sky filtered in and out of his vision. Medical staff passed by in their birdlike masks; others held rags to their exposed noses, their skin marred by smudges of smoke as the stench of burning tar permeated the air.

Smell their fear. Revel in their fear.

Panic of his own clutched as Jason's heart as he took in this vision…another hallucination? He didn't take the time to wonder as he forced his feet to move and shoved his way down the hall, breath coming out in ragged tears as black smoke filled his lungs.

By the time he reached the end of the hall, his chest hurt from holding his breath, but the panic had faded to a kind of wary fascination.

Sickness is your sickness, the voice mocked. *How you long to be part of their world.*

"What is this?" Jason whispered. One hand held the door to his lab open, the other tempted to reach out and touch the closest figure, with her smudged scrubs and scarred leather mask. But she turned away from him and disappeared into the smoke, which trembled back into a hard off-white wall.

After a moment of staring at the space, Jason took a step back and faded into the shadows as well.

By the time Jason reached the lab, his lungs were clear and his eyes took in only the familiar sights of his office. A glance through the window showed doctors and nurses he'd known for years passing by in their normal hospital wear. He shook his head at himself, internally laughing at his moment of panic. There were no doctors wearing beak-masks, no smoke in the halls. Just St. Peters Hospital, as he'd known it for the past decade. The stress truly was getting to him.

"Just get to work and maybe call the shrink afterwards," he told himself, and did just that.

It was three hours later when the lab door opened, and a familiar face appeared.

"Roger! Good to see you. What brings you down here?" Jason asked, setting down his safety glasses and looking up at his friend. The plump doctor was clearly distressed.

"You've heard about the quarantine?"

Jason nodded, his good mood instantly vanishing. News of an extremely ill patient had reached the lab almost instantly upon the man's arrival. At the time he hadn't thought much of it. Patients came in every day dying of something horrible, though he couldn't discount just how worried everyone seemed to be over this one. Not having seen the patient or his charts himself, Jason could only wait to cast his own judgment.

"Yes, in the ICU. One of the techs told me just a little bit ago that a patient came in with a strange virus and was bleeding profusely, but I haven't seen his bloodwork yet. I'm waiting on the doctors to bring it down once they have the quarantine set up."

"And what do you think they will find?"

The way Roger asked the question, with his arms crossed and his tone accusing, had Jason's eyes narrowing. He crossed his own arms. "Why don't you tell me?"

Roger sighed and took a seat across from Jason. "I read the preliminary report on this patient and spoke to a couple nurses before I examined him myself. This patient, a man named Keven Carlson, I'm worried he might be our Patient Zero."

The first in the war to rid the world of vermin.

Though the declaration filled Jason with anticipation, he asked, "What...what do you mean?"

"I mean, what we know so far is frightening, Jason. And I haven't told anyone yet, but I'm starting to wonder if I know more about this than I should." Roger sighed again and leaned back in the chair, adjusting his tie nervously. "He came in complaining of a fever, headaches, and vomiting and defecating blood. His skin looked jaundiced as well, so he was admitted. Before nurses could even blood test him he began bleeding from his nose, eyes, and mouth. Rivers of blood, Jason. They are still cleaning up the ER. The patient was transferred to the isolation room immediately."

Fingers drumming lightly on the tabletop, Jason listened intently, his interest growing with each new piece of information. He wanted to see this patient, examine him, determine what sickness pulsed through his veins. "I'll handle his blood samples myself, see what I can find."

"That's fine, but I need to know what you already know about this."

Confused, and a little suspicious, Jason rose. Roger followed. "What are you saying, Roger?"

"I remember what we saw in that initial blood sample, Jason. Tessa's sample. I told you then it looked like it was mimicking yellow fever. And now this patient is showing the same signs. Jaundice, headaches, body aches, fever, vomiting, bleeding from orifices." Roger ticked off each symptom on his fingers. "Is there something I need to know about? Did something happen with that sample?"

"Of course not," Jason replied immediately, hating how defensive his voice sounded. "I took care of it."

Suspicion bloomed in the doctor's eyes. "What does that mean, you took care of it?"

"Are you doubting me?" Anger twisted in Jason's gut, a rage he felt slicing through his body and turning to ice behind his eyes. "Yellow fever is caused by mosquitoes, Roger. And many people are vaccinated against it these days. Besides, it's most commonly known in tropical countries, like Africa and South America."

"And Savannah," Roger replied quietly, his stare never leaving Jason.

An enemy in the way against the vermin.

"Get out of my lab," Jason demanded. The words formed before he knew what he was saying, but he welcomed them all the same. "I won't tolerate you accusing me of…whatever it is you're accusing me of. Get out, or I'll have you removed."

For a moment Roger only stood there, still staring. Then he relented and took a step back. "I hope I'm wrong. But if I'm not, and whatever this man has begins to spread, I won't hesitate to report you to the board."

Taking the final word with him, Roger left the lab, wanting to run away from the man he considered a good friend, but worried that doing so would trigger the predator he was leaving behind.

CHAPTER 16

That night, after most of the day-shift doctors and nurses had gone home, Jason slipped out of the lab. His feet led him to the ICU, where the quarantine had been set up. It didn't take him long to suit up into one of the isolation suits and ease his way into the room where their alleged Patient Zero was resting.

The man lying upon the bed was strapped to so many monitors Jason wasn't sure where the tubes began and ended. A steady array of beeps sounded throughout the small room. Perusing each machine, Jason nodded to himself as he made a pass around the bed, concocting his own diagnosis at each monitor before finally coming to a stop at the end of the bed. His hands gripped the railing, eyes taking in the sight.

The man was still, breath shallow, skin yellow and almost... mushy, Jason pondered with a frown, as though the body would melt away at a moment's notice and leave behind a pulpy mass of bone and blood. The tubes around his nose were tinted red from what Jason assumed were several nosebleeds since being admitted, and there were scabs around the man's mouth and ears, staining his red hair.

Red hair. Recognition dawned on Jason as he realized who he was staring at. This was the man who had knocked him down at the football game not so long ago. The big, burly brute with fiery red hair and an arrogance that spurred the desire within Jason to create a disease that would take him out.

We need a new plague.

"How the mighty have fallen," he muttered, knuckles whitening as his fingers tightened around the bed railing.

"Jason?"

Spinning around, Jason saw Doctor Mac Williams standing behind him dressed in a matching biohazard suit. "Mac," he greeted with a nod, not at all surprised by now smooth and unaffected he sounded. He'd been feeling calm and collected recently, completely in control of himself.

"What are you doing in here?"

Still just as smoothly, he replied, "We've been processing the blood specimens for this patient and trying to nail down a diagnosis. The samples are unlike any I've ever seen before, so I thought I'd come in here and take a look. Thought maybe I could better process things if I knew firsthand what we are dealing with."

Not needing to read the chart, he continued with his story. "The patient came in with a headache, body aches, and blood loss, correct?"

Dr. Williams nodded and stepped up next to the other man. "We initially suspected a flu of some sort. God knows we've had enough of them recently to see some nasty stuff. This patient, Keven Carlson, came in complaining of a headache, fever, and defecating blood. Within a few hours his organs were starting to shut down and he was bleeding internally. He was initially jaundiced, but it worsened to what you see now, which was when we began suspecting yellow fever."

"Dr. Willcox mentioned that," Jason mused. "A little fast for yellow fever to progress though, isn't it?"

"You'd think." The doctor sighed. "Actually, Dr. Willcox suggested it, said he was already running some tests. I don't know why that was his first thought, all things considered."

The enemy in this war, becoming too rash and unreliable.

Jason wanted to fume, to find his old friend and smash his head against the wall. It was a struggle to remain calm. "Has this patient traveled out of the country? Anywhere he may have contracted the virus?"

"Not that we know of. His girlfriend's the one who called 911, said he hadn't done any traveling since last year, when he went to Maine. Not exactly a sub-tropical climate breeding yellow fever-infested mosquitos." The doctor shrugged. "Then again, we don't know when he first contracted the virus, if that's what it is. All we know is what you see, so all can do right now is treat the symptoms and hope for a diagnosis soon. Speaking of, have you found anything?"

"Not yet. We're working on it though."

You don't need to find anything, came the rough voice in his mind, sending a chill over Jason's skin. *You know what ails this peasant. You know what kills him.*

Next to him, Dr. Williams frowned. "You okay, Jason?"

"Yeah, yeah." He shook his head to rid it of the voice. "Just frustrated is all. I should get back to the lab and run some more tests. If anything changes, let me know."

He turned to leave, but paused mid-step when he heard shouting from down the hall. Within seconds a group of doctors and nurses dressed in quarantine suits appeared, racing down the hall with a gurney. Upon that stretcher lay a woman with red-stained bandages covering her eyes and mouth.

"Shit." Dr. Williams raced for the door, yanking it open to allow them entrance and immediately going to work.

Unable to help, Jason made to leave, edging around the nurses on his way to the door. He couldn't help but glance down at the woman as he passed. Her skin was yellow, blouse covered with blood from when she's apparently vomited earlier. When her eyes fluttered open briefly, Jason saw they too were pale and yellow— and the sight caused his stomach to clench in excitement.

His virus was spreading.

Torn between the desire to stay and watch this woman bleed

and the need to let the doctors do their work, Jason merely stood there, taking in the scene. Only when he was bumped out of the way did he finally move. He slipped to the back, unable to resist one final glance over his shoulder. As he did, a doctor looked up, their eyes locking for the briefest of moments.

And in that moment Jason felt a stirring, a lust deep within for the man's fear. The doctor was afraid. He was unsure. He was resolute in the fact he could not save this woman. The suit shifted before Jason's eyes, warping into the bird-like mask he'd seen before, leather and beak and glass fogged with dark smoke. Then it was just a quarantine suit, and a frightened doctor.

Blowing out a heavy breath, Jason turned and left the room, and the bleeding woman, behind.

*

Two days later, Jason sat at his computer, eyes scanning lab results but not really seeing anything. These results told him everything they needed to know. Everything he already knew.

Keven Carlson wasn't sick with yellow fever. In person, it appeared he was, with all the right symptoms. But on paper, he was infected with a virus no one had ever seen before, with its roots in an old disease but growing new limbs of its own.

Elevated liver enzymes, anemia, abnormal white blood cells, signs of kidney failure. No, Keven Carlson wasn't sick with yellow fever. He was sick with something far worse—RYF-2. The illness not yet revealed, Resurrect Fever not yet made public.

A knock at his closed door broke his attention from the screen. Lifting his gaze to the small window looking out into the workspace, Jason saw Roger and another man standing in the lab. *His* lab. A cold calm settled in Jason's body as he rose and stalked to the door slowly, calculating their expressions. Frowning, stiff... nervous.

"Gentlemen," he greeted after opening the door, nodding at Roger while shaking the third man's hand.

"Good to see you again, Jason," Gary Day replied. "I'm sorry I couldn't make it to your welcoming party. Just got back into town."

"Just in time for the chaos." Jason looked the smaller man up and down, not at all intimidated by the fact that the person standing before him was one of the board directors. He gestured for them to sit in the chairs on the other side of his desk. "How can I help you?"

Roger started to reply, only to be cut off by the director. "We've had eleven patients brought in over the last two days. That makes a total of twelve patients, including the first, Keven Carlson, in the quarantine room. Twelve patients in seven days and we are no closer to figuring out what's wrong with them. We're trying to figure out the correlation between them, where they were, what they were doing when they first realized they were sick, but we are clearly running out of time here."

Jason waited, but Gary was finished, staring at him expectantly. "We're doing the best we can down here with the samples provided."

"I don't need the best, Jason. I need better than that. I need answers."

He needs. He needs. He needs.

Jason leaned back in the chair. The voice mocked him, angered him. "You need to give me longer to figure this out. Viral cultures take time. You know this. Medicine can't always be rushed to fit a picture-perfect timetable."

In response, it was his friend who spoke. "Time is not a luxury we can afford right now. The way Keven Carlson is progressing, he won't last the rest of the week if we don't figure something out. I'm not sure why he is getting sicker so much faster than the others, but my guess is because he's the first. Patient Zero, as I told you when he first came in."

"We're doing what we can," Jason repeated. His eyes narrowed at Roger, who attempted to shrink back in his seat at the direct and menacing glare.

Not noticing the friction, Gary added, "We can't afford to have this get out of control. Not just for these patients, but for the public. You know how the public reacts to things like this. And with the media already getting their hooks in the story, it could blow up bigger than we can control."

A selfish plea for help, the spirit reminded him. *He cares for himself, not the ill and weak.*

Jason nodded at the demon's words. To the men before him, it looked like he was contemplating the director's statement, rather than inwardly scorning it. "People get sick all the time, Gary. There's no need to fear public outcry."

"This is turning into something much bigger than a few sick people," Roger insisted. "This is becoming an epidemic, according to the media, and we both know that's all that matters, what the media says. People will latch on to that. The media picked up on it early because one of the patients collapsed in a grocery store, and even have security footage of the woman bleeding out in the middle of the cereal aisle. Things like that make for great TV when people are eating dinner and putting the kids to bed. Everyone loves a good disaster story. Now they are already blowing it up, scaring everyone into thinking some super virus is going around Jacksonville."

The words hung in the air, thick and cold and brimming with a malice-filled future. Jason felt them seep into him. They invigorated him, fed the beast thriving within, reminded him how much he loved the thrill of the diagnosis, the mystery of the disease.

"A super virus," he repeated slowly, turning the words over in his mind. "A plague, one might say."

"Let's hope not," Gary replied hurriedly. "We need to stop this now, before it becomes a plague. And, more importantly, we need to keep that word, *plague*, out of people's minds. Otherwise it's going to be chaos the likes of which this city has never seen."

Chaos, how we will bask in its beauty.

Though he agreed, his heart beating against the thrill of such a future, Jason said, "You'll have your results soon."

CHAPTER 17

Time he never even thought to track passed before Jason finally allowed himself to leave the lab. Hours spent pouring over test results from twelve sick patients. Minutes spent printing them out in preparation for the doctors. Seconds spent dismissing any worries over what those results said.

Nodding his goodnight to the evening crew, Jason slung his bag over his shoulder and walked through the halls slowly, taking in each and every scene. The nurses gathered in a small huddle, worry plastered across their weary faces. A duo of doctors comparing charts, hands scrubbing over tired faces. Patients tucked away in their rooms, watching the activity just outside their doors through wide eyes. Visitors with expressions of regret, wondering what they were risking coming to the hospital with a dozen men and women under quarantine.

Shaking his head at them all, Jason adjusted his bag up higher on his shoulder, one hand holding the strap protectively and his body angled so it wouldn't brush up against anyone or thing. He walked through the glass double doors—and froze at the blinding assault that greeted him. One hand lifted to shield his eyes, the other to block the cameras shoved in his face. His name was being shouted at him from all directions, along with a barrage of questions.

Is it true? they yelled, desperately seeking insight into what lay beyond the hospital doors.

What is the patients' diagnosis? they demanded to know, as though they had the right to such information.

Unable to get past the reporters, Jason lowered his arm and dropped his bag to his waist in front of him, focusing on the petite, blonde woman nearly stepping on his toes as she lifted a microphone to his mouth. "Mr. Waters! Twelve patients have been admitted to the hospital in the past week with severe and frightening symptoms, including internal and external bleeding. Is it true doctors are suspecting an outbreak of a virus or bacteria no one can diagnose, perhaps something that has never been seen before, or hasn't been seen for many years?"

Jason frowned, though inwardly he felt satisfaction purring throughout his body. "Many patients have been admitted to the hospital for a variety of reasons."

"So it's true?" the reporter surmised, her brown eyes drilling into him in an attempt to get him to talk. "Have you personally worked on these patients' results?"

"I'm not at liberty to say. Patients have rights, Miss, regardless of your intrusive questions."

She waited, silent among the roaring crowd, but Jason offered no further insight. Pressing on, she continued, "Is there anything you can tell us about the patients, or what they are suffering from?"

His head cocked slightly to the side as he stared down at the woman. Something in his expression made her pause and attempt to slink backward, but there was nowhere to go. "Does it worry you, what they might be suffering from?"

At this response, the crowd quieted, a unified unease both confusing and silencing them. Cameras continued to roll, but no questions were asked. A chill shivered through every reporter, every cameraman, surrounding Jason, until they all felt cold and clammy in the presence of the only man who could give them the answers they sought. Only now, they weren't sure they wanted those answers after all.

They seek a truth they cannot handle, spoke the voice of his consciousness. *Give them the fear they crave.*

"Are you afraid?" Jason asked the blonde reporter, stepping closer and forcing her to step back. "Are you afraid of what may lurk on the other side of the hospital doors?"

His blue eyes pierced hers, a challenge and a warning. The reporter swallowed hard, trapped by his stare as she answered, "Yes."

Jason blinked. A slow blink, accompanied by an itchy slide against his skin. "Good," he replied, enjoying the fear slowly spreading across her face. "You should be."

A sense of euphoria followed Jason home, a welcoming acceptance of what he'd done, the fear he'd fostered…the panic he was soon to nurture. Seeing the gruff and formidable Keven Carlson so helpless on the bed reminded him why he'd done this— because people needed to remember their place in the world, to know how easily it could all be taken away by someone with a little more knowledge, and a little more power.

As he made dinner, a simple meal of steak and asparagus, Jason flipped through the television channels until he found the news. He left it on in the background while cooking. Stories of a stolen car, a dog that rescued a child from a pool, something about the war overseas. He ignored them all until one word caught his ear.

Epidemic.

Turning the burner off, Jason looked to the TV, seeing the petite blonde stick who'd attempted to interview him earlier. She was dressed the same, hair and makeup perfectly done up, but there was a look in her eye he recognized. A look he'd put there so few hours ago.

She was afraid, and he reveled in her fear.

"That's right, Janet," the woman was saying to the anchor as she gestured to the hospital behind her. His hospital. "At this point, Jacksonville residents are being advised to *not* leave the city, while non-residents are potentially being warned to avoid traveling through the city until this mystery illness is properly diagnosed and treated."

Jason lifted a brow, chewing on a piece of steak. He hadn't heard of the advisory, but then, he hadn't paid much attention to the news lately.

"An advisory?" the other anchorman repeated. "Is it a bit early for an advisory? There have been twelve patients, but so far all of them are alive and being treated."

"A dozen patients so far," the reporter corrected, her tone solemn and her eyes wide. "We don't know yet what we're dealing with, but even those at the hospital are concerned. I spoke with lab manager Jason Waters earlier this evening. I'm sure you'll remember Waters from the attack by Tessa Taylor last year. He has recently returned to work and had this to say about the recent epidemic."

Amused, Jason watched the screen flicker and change until he was staring at himself. Not himself, he realized with a small amount of worry. Oh, that was his face, his voice, his clothes. But there was something...different about him. A strange calmness, a cold exterior, the look of a man who didn't give a damn about the people in the hospital behind him, but was nearly orgasmic at the sight of the reporter's apparent terror. Even his voice was changed, he noted, swallowing a piece of asparagus. Level, indifferent, and then...full of danger.

The anchors were visibly rattled when the reporter turned the segment back to them. Jason merely chuckled, until the one named Janet added, "Maybe Tessa Taylor wasn't the only one possessed in that lab. Seems Mr. Waters could use a good night's rest." His grip on the fork tightened and he waited for more, but the anchors laughed to themselves and moved on.

"Impressive."

The voice that had startled him the first time, this time made him smile. Slowly Jason turned and nodded to Tessa, who was standing in the doorway to the kitchen. "You're back."

"What makes you think I ever left? I have work to do wherever I go."

The response had him glancing over at the TV again, where he watched a banner slide across the screen announcing a murder—the prime suspects being Tessa and Braden Taylor. The Taylor Sibling Slaughters had struck Jacksonville again, with nary a trace of the killers to be found. The only evidence left behind of their presence was the headless corpse bleeding out in an empty bathtub, and the little girl confessing to police what her father had done to her.

Less than man, less than animal, indeed.

Not at all bothered by the news, Tessa sauntered in, stealing a piece of asparagus from his plate. The simple move had him completely forgetting the anchorwoman speaking in the background. His eyes followed the movement, watching her lips wrap around the spear, imagining those lips wrapped around something else.

"None of that," she said with a lifted brow, breaking him from a daydream she could apparently read in his expression. "We're in this together now."

"In what?"

She shook his head at his confusion and stared over at him with interest. "Do you really not know what has happened? Do you even know who you are anymore?"

"Of course I do. Jason Waters, virus creator extraordinaire." His chest puffed out playfully, even as his blood warmed at the self-professed title.

"Interesting." Tessa moved closer, sliding her hand up his forearm, fingers dancing against his flesh. "You must like him."

A dark soul hidden beneath a bright surface.

The voice surprised Jason, who jerked back. "Who are you talking to?" But he knew the answer, and when Tessa merely smiled, he knew she did as well. She was talking to the one who followed him home from Savannah, the one who fed on his desire to fuel sickness and disease, the one he welcomed into his heart and soul.

"A partnership," she continued, patting him on the cheek before heading for the door. "He took from you your pain, your scars, your fear. And, in return, you gave him the world."

It was only after she left that he realized he never actually felt her skin against his own, yet her touch had stirred up something dark deep within him. He knew who he was. He was a powerful man, a dangerous one, who would extinguish the lives of those who didn't serve them. Before, he'd been weak. Now, he'd found a way to survive.

Yes, he would co-exist. And yes, he would give the darkness within the entire world.

CHAPTER 18

They were waiting for him when he arrived at work the next day.

Jason eyed the group as he entered, five men and two women looking far too serious this early in the morning. He set down his jacket hesitantly and looked to the two familiar faces. "Gary, Roger. Is everything okay?"

"You tell us, Jason," Roger replied coolly, arms crossed over his bulky stomach. "We saw the news last night. Pretty sure everyone in the city saw it. Why would you say such a thing?"

Doing his best to appear concerned, Jason lifted a shoulder. "People need to know to be afraid. This is a concerning illness we're dealing with."

"Not like this," Gary countered. "You know the protocol for handling the media, Jason. I don't understand what happened last night. What you did not only made the hospital look bad, but it fueled panic throughout the city. Our hospital alone had a major spike in ER visits last night, many of which were nothing more than a case of the sniffles."

Jason started to reply but paused, one simply word catching his attention. "...Many?" He saw the moment recognition set in, realization of what was said and revealed. "Many patients had the sniffles, and the others?"

Gary cleared his throat, glancing over at Roger before admitting, "Thirteen patients had the beginning symptoms of our mystery illness. They were admitted to the quarantine zone. We now have so many patients we've had to change the fifth floor into an isolation zone. Hence why the CDC became involved."

"Ah." Jason sat back, hiding a grin. "So that's who you fine men and women are." He glanced at them each in turn, five strangers in suits and pencil skirts appearing more suspicious than worried. Before they could introduce themselves, Jason continued, "So some good came of last night after all. Those thirteen patients could still be at home, infecting their loved ones. Or they could have gone to work today, infecting their co-workers."

"So you want us to believe this was some act of civic duty?" Roger's tone was as sarcastic as his expression.

"Mr. Waters," one of the women said before an argument could be had. "My name is Tina Burns. I and my colleagues here are with the CDC. Doctor Day and Doctor Willcox contacted us in regards to this epidemic. They, as well as the CDC, have some concerns."

Jason appreciated the older woman speaking up, taking charge in a room dominated by men. But his appreciation ended there. When he spoke next, it was with disdain and boredom. "Concerns about what, Ms. Burns?"

"About what you are doing in this lab," the man next to her replied. He was tall and thin, with thick black hair and glasses to match.

"We would like to search the lab," Burns added.

Indignation flared within Jason. "I don't think—"

"It was not a request, Mr. Waters."

They were staring him down, or trying too, Jason thought with a hidden grin. Unbeknownst to them, he'd been expecting Roger—an enemy in his war—to pull a stunt like this and had prepared accordingly. They would find nothing incriminating in his lab, for the sample was safely tucked away in a small cabinet in his bedroom at home, where he'd stored it just last night. Any files he had on his tests were moved to his home computer in a locked file, and the materials he'd used to create RYF-2 had already gone through the hospital's incinerator.

"Go ahead," he welcomed with a sweep of his arm. "I'll wait here."

All but one of the CDC employees began their search, donning latex gloves before spreading out. He barely paid attention to their invasions into his laboratory. Instead his focus was on the friend he now considered a traitor.

"You brought in the CDC, thinking you would stop me from some heinous act when you have no proof I have even done anything wrong."

"I saw you on the news last night," Roger answered defensively. "We've spoken about this epidemic before. Something is wrong, Jason."

"Yes, something is." Jason wondered if the doctor realized how easy it would be for him to reveal the truth about the blood sample, that the esteemed Dr. Willcox stole a sample from Jason's home and hid it away for nine months, and ran additional tests that were never approved. Roger seemed to have forgotten his part in this story, but Jason was willing to bide his time and wait for the right moment to strike.

"When they find nothing wrong with my lab, I'll expect an apology from you."

Rather than an apology, Roger replied, "Jason, I don't know what's going on with you lately. Maybe you weren't ready to come back. Maybe you need to talk to someone again about the attack. But whatever it is, we are concerned you might not be the best person to be handling these cases."

"The CDC has concerns as well," Burns put in. "With nearly thirty patients exhibiting signs of this unknown disease, we need the top experts in the field working around the clock on treatments and research. We cannot have anyone in the way."

They doubt, said the darkness within.

We will make them bow before us, was his response.

We gave them disease, and we will save them from it, the demon agreed.

"I'm working on finding the pathogen causing this. There's your big mystery, *Doctor* Willcox, the big suspicious reason I've been so tight-lipped about my work. You said it yourself: people are panicking. The last thing I want to do is claim to be working on a cure and get people's hopes up when it takes longer than expected, or doesn't work at all," Jason finally decided to say. "I figured, if I could isolate it, I could send it to the CDC to help find a cure. A cure," he repeated, "to help these people. And I am close to figuring out what this illness is, and, when I do, I'll know how to treat it. A few more days and you'll have your answers, provided you actually let me do my job."

Roger didn't reply, choosing to step back and wander around the lab instead while it was being searched. The investigation lasted for just over an hour, and, as Jason expected, nothing incriminating was found.

And, also as expected, no apology was offered.

*

Roger felt like he was sneaking around the hospital as he made his way up a floor to a colleague's office. He was really only trying to hide from one person, but worried someone may spread the word that he was in the office of one Doctor Suzanne Hart.

Suzanne was considered one of the foremost experts in infectious diseases. She had witnessed firsthand the horrors illness and disease played upon the body, had healed the ill across the world, and lost just as many as she saved. Her time with the WHO taught her that some sicknesses could not be healed, but not trying at all was worse than letting people die. And so she spent her days researching plagues of the past, hoping to pull some part of history to the present in order to heal those in the future. Her papers were published in medical journals the world over, her teachings bringing in doctors and students by the thousands.

Which was why Roger was now in her office. He needed to hear her wisdom, needed to seek her advice before the entire city was in peril.

"Suzanne," he greeted as he entered, shutting the door behind him. "I'm glad I could catch you before you left for your trip."

"Of course, though I'm disappointed to say my trip to the Virgin Islands has been postponed for now." She gestured toward the chair on the other side of her desk. Roger sat, taking in the older woman. Her hair was a gorgeous dark red, artificial, no doubt, judging by the wrinkles lining her eyes and forehead. The locks were styled in an elegant bob that framed her slim face and brought out the bright blue of her eyes. She wore little makeup, but dressed in a business suit and heels. Roger knew she was nearing seventy, yet she seemed much younger, though no less intimidating.

This was a woman whose very presence exuded intelligence.

"So I assume you know why I'm here."

Suzanne nodded, her lips pressed together in a tight line. For a moment she stared at her hands, which were clasped together. "I do," she answered gravely. "I've been looking over the tests and results, and I went to see several of the patients myself. With the advisory to not leave the city, I decided to cancel my vacation and help out here instead. I don't think I've left the hospital in three days." She smiled, but there was no light in the expression. She was tired, worried, and nervous, and it showed.

Not wanting to waste time, Roger nodded in encouragement. "What have you found?"

"They just keep coming in. We now have forty-nine patients all showing the same signs. Fever, body aches, vomiting, and, of course, bleeding from various orifices. So far only one patient, our Patient Zero, seems to have progressed to having his organs essentially shut down, though the others are rapidly developing jaundice and blood in their stool. Lab results have been mixed, and confusing, as you know. It's almost as though something doesn't want us to get the results."

Roger's attention peaked at that. "You think someone has been tampering with the results?"

"Oh, no." Suzanne waved a hand with a small chuckle. "Just my way of saying I don't understand what's happening. I know what it *feels* like, but not what it is."

"What does it feel like?"

Suzanne took in a deep breath and let it out on a sigh. "It feels...well, it feels like yellow fever, which is crazy, I know. But the symptoms...they all lead back to yellow fever, with one exception. Our Patient Zero, Keven Carlson, this virus is attacking his organs. We have already had to remove his spleen. Now it looks like his kidneys are deteriorating. Not failing, just...dissolving, you might say. *That* isn't a yellow fever attribute. If it were yellow fever, I'd say it is a mutated form. A worse form, as it were, something more akin to a hemorrhagic fever. Something our modern medicine can't quite figure out. We can treat the symptoms for comfort, but right now, that's all we're treating. Worse, Carlson isn't the only one with organ failure. Everyone admitted the same week as him are all developing the same extreme symptoms. I'm worried it's only a matter of time before the rest of them have the same problems."

Roger knew all that, but it frightened him to hear the truth coming from Suzanne, one of the most respected medical professionals the nation had ever seen. But he wanted to know more despite his reservations, and so he pursued the subject. "What do you know about yellow fever?"

"Just about everything." She said it with resignation, a celebrated doctor for once defeated by her knowledge.

"What can you tell me about it?"

"Probably nothing you don't already know. It's a virus that shows up within three to six days of exposure, usually in the form of a fever and nausea, perhaps body aches. Mimicking the flu, mostly, or malaria. It can even be misdiagnosed as dengue fever or something similar, for those in the more tropical regions. Most patients don't even get past this point before the virus clears up on its own. Those who don't see more severe symptoms. Jaundice, vomiting, blood in the vomit and stool, bleeding from the eyes, nose, and mouth. Patients can recover from this, but some have lifelong organ damage."

He did know most of that, but it helped him work through his thoughts as he listened to the older doctor speak. "I ordered a lab workup to test for yellow fever."

Suzanne sat back and eyed Roger curiously, seeing something in his expression even he wasn't aware of. "You suspected yellow fever? Early enough to have already ordered a workup?" When Roger only returned her stare, her eyes narrowed. "Do you know something I don't?"

He didn't want to express his concerns without having all the facts. For some reason, he feared that doing so would give Jason the advantage he needed to truly bury him. So he deflected, while trying to get more information from the vastly educated doctor. "No, of course not. I just remember seeing a television show about yellow fever recently. Specifically, the yellow fever outbreak in Savannah in the 1800s."

"Ah, yes." Suzanne nodded, her eyes drifting to a blank space on the wall above Roger's head as her mind traveled. "That was a dark time with a devastating plague. People died by the dozens, hundreds. Some reports said that doctors were seeing as many as one hundred patients a day, not even able to treat the virus, only the symptoms, trying to keep people comfortable until they could find a cure."

"What did they try?"

Suzanne laughed, the sound dry and incredulous. "Things that by today's standards seem almost barbaric. Medicines containing arsenic, sulfuric acid, belladonna. It's rumored they even fed patients hot tar thinking it would kill the virus. When that clearly didn't work, they began burning tar in the streets, believing that the smoke would keep the plague away, and attempting to sanitize ballast stones from the ships, since the virus began at the ports. Eventually they began isolating patients to avoid the spread of the fever, while others turned to drugs, alcohol, and religion. I suppose the one positive thing that came out of the plague was that they began paying closer attention to sanitation, and cleaned up the city to avoid stagnant water and other breeding grounds for mosquitoes. Cleaning out drains, whitewashing old wood, cleaning up rotting or molding vegetation, and so forth."

She started to speak more on the sanitation methods, but Roger cut her off. "You keep saying *plague*," he emphasized. "Do you think that's what we are looking at here?"

"It's possible." With a nod, the other doctor thought for a moment before continuing. "If we look at Savannah, for example. People began getting sick, no one knew the cause, a quarantine was called. Back then, anyone traveling from Savannah were quarantined in cities like Jacksonville, and farther north in South Carolina, in order to prevent the spread. Are we not doing nearly the same thing now? We have a virus we cannot truly explain, that we cannot treat or cure as of yet, and that has put our entire hospital essentially in lockdown. We are telling people not to leave the city, and other cities are telling their residents not to travel through ours. The CDC has set up camp in the hospital and is threatening to quarantine the entire city. Part of me fears that by the end of this, Jacksonville will be what Savannah was feared to be after it was all over—a black hole of sorts, a place of death."

Her words rang through Roger's thoughts. He'd had similar concerns. "How do we cure this?" he asked, returning his gaze to hers, but she only shook her head sadly.

"Of all the answers I have, for that question, I am just as lost as you."

CHAPTER 19

Roger left the doctor's office confident they were closer to figuring out the source of the illness, but fearful of what the discovery would cost. Such worry was written across his face, though there were none around to see it.

Or so he deceived himself into believing.

Around the opposite corner, Jason waited, listening to the portly doctor amble away. He'd tracked the man's whereabouts throughout the day, watching him first leave the lab, then examine the patients in isolation, get some paperwork done at his desk, and eventually make his way to Suzanne Hart's office. Roger had shared his fears with the specialist, incited her curiosity and her concern.

And now she would suffer the consequences for her colleague's intellectual invasion.

Once Roger had disappeared down the hall, Jason rounded the corner and headed for the specialist's office. His walk was slow, purposeful, and yet brimming with anticipation. When he entered the office, Suzanne glanced up from a pile of paperwork, her eyes narrowing when he closed the door behind him and stood, waiting for her to speak.

"Mr. Waters," she said cautiously. "How can I help you?"

He took a seat before answering. "I was curious what you thought of the test results the CDC has come up with. They were kind enough to share their findings with me, so I assumed they did with you as well, given your in-depth studies on disease. I figured, with your studies in infectious diseases, maybe you would have some insight into what's causing these patients to fall ill."

Leaning back in her cushioned chair, Suzanne frowned, unsure where this conversation was going and not trusting his motives were pure, judging by the gleam in his eye and the smoothness to his voice. "Wouldn't that be your job, Mr. Waters, to analyze the results brought to you from all of our patients?"

"I suppose it would be."

Silence befell the duo, uncomfortable and tinted with an air of growing worry. Finally, Suzanne shifted and picked up a pen, a move Jason noted was filled with nerves and tension. "If you truly want to know what I think…I think it's a mutated form of yellow fever. I don't know how it came about. I've never seen anything like this before, though I suppose it's possible. Viruses mutate all the time. It's just a matter of figuring out how, and how to treat it. But, I did learn this morning that doctors and researchers have traced this illness back to a football game a couple weeks ago. About eighty percent of our patients were there. The other twenty percent are either family members or co-workers. Coincidence? Possibly, but unlikely."

A football game ending in death, Jason mused. His human soul barely recalled attending a game, though he certainly remembered being knocked down by a drunken thug. The demon within shivered at the memory, heating its host's body with the pleasure of infection. "Someone had the virus, spread it to the attendees."

"Yes," the doctor said on a near whisper, "*someone* had the virus, indeed."

"And if it is spreading quickly, it is likely an airborne virus."

"That is my suspicion, yes," Suzanne confessed. "Though how our Patient Zero contracted it in the first place is still a mystery, given there have been no other reports of the virus anywhere other than Jacksonville."

Nodding, Jason rose abruptly and stuck out his hand. "Thank

you for meeting with me, Doctor Hart. This has been most educational."

Hesitantly, Suzanne looked from his hand to his eyes. Something in his expression warned her what would happen should she refuse his offer. Slowly, almost unwillingly, she too reached out, lightly grasping his hand with her own. But that light touch was all he needed.

It started in her fingers, a cold piercing sensation, before traveling up her arm, cramping in her back and shoulders. "What..."

Words died in a bubble of blood that burst from her lips. Fever instantly racked her body, sweat forming along her brow as thick red liquid seeped from her ears, the corners of her eyes. Doubling over, Suzanne collapsed on her desk, a strained squeal-like sound escaping her tight throat as agonizing pain chewed at her insides.

"Curious, isn't it?" Jason said, still holding her hand as he leaned over her shuddering form. "You spend your entire life studying disease, only to be destroyed by the one you cannot figure out." Leaning in closer still, he whispered, "This is *my* disease. *My* plague. Look how fast I can destroy a person. How fast I can destroy any who try to stand in my way."

Releasing her, Jason glanced down at the needle tucked into his bloody palm before dropping it in his pocket. He rolled his shoulders, feeling the weight of an unseen soul bearing down on him, giving strength to a disease cultivated by his own two hands. An example of what he could do, and how fast he could do it if he truly wanted to speed up the deathly process.

"But where's the fun in that," he murmured, staring down at the woman's still, bloody form, her organs liquefied inside her. There was no time to relish in her panic, to hear her pleas for salvation or watch her body slowly waste away. The fast death was boring, anticlimactic. The real fun was in watching them suffer in sickness.

Turning away, Jason shoved his hand in his pocket to hide the blood and walked away, making sure the door was locked behind him.

*

The isolation zone was quiet, an entire floor in quarantine. Doctors spoke in hushed tones over the hum of monitors and coughing of patients. Rooms were packed with the ill and ailing, some spilling out in the halls, the entire fifth floor overrun with an overflow continuing to grow by the hour. Paramedics and nurses brought patients up steadily, unable to keep up with the constant demand for more beds, more medicine, more cleanup of blood trailing along the floor. So much demand, they'd begun turning patients away, the CDC demanding neighboring Jacksonville hospitals dedicate their own floors for isolation and begin admitting the sick.

This all went unnoticed by the man who'd been there the longest, the man they all called Patient Zero. In his unconscious state, he never knew he was the one blamed for starting it all. He hadn't woken in days—and wouldn't wake again.

While nurses tended to patients all around the bed in the back of a room sectioned off by a plastic drape, Keven's body began to shiver. His already sallow and spongey skin sweated out a thick fever, separating from muscle and bone. Cracked lips parted to allow for shallow, gasping breaths to accompany agonizing pain the ailing man felt even in sleep.

Within a body ravaged by disease, organs shuddered. A weak heart pumped blood through veins no longer able to contain the life force. Slow beats, but enough to give power to a flow of blood erupting from every orifice. Red dripped from ears, nose, eyes, genitals, what was left of the anemic man formerly known as Keven Carlson pouring onto the hospital floor.

CHAPTER 20

Blood washed down the drain, swirling in the white porcelain sink as Jason scrubbed his hands clean. He hummed to himself while working the soap over his skin. A smile etched its way across his face at the memory of Suzanne's muffled scream, the sound she made as the virus sped its way through her bloodstream and attacked her organs. She thought she could best him. Her arrogance was her death.

She would not be the only one to pay such a price.

Finally clean, Jason bleached down the sink and floor, making sure no traces of blood remained, then stepped out of the small bathroom located in the back of his laboratory. A muffled curse escaped when he nearly ran into Sam.

"Careful," he said, when he really wanted to reach inside the man and squeeze the blood from his heart.

"Sorry," the young intern replied, out of breath. "I just got a call you need to hear." Before Jason could give him the go-ahead, Sam pushed on. "Patient Zero, Keven Carlson, he just died. Bled out all over the floor after complete organ failure. He's the first, Mr. Waters. And somehow the media already heard all about it and they are going crazy outside. Cops are just barely keeping them from barging inside."

Jason blew out a breath, emotions torn. The side of him still clinging to ration said this was bad, that the virus had reached the moment when chaos would erupt if it wasn't handled properly.

The part of him already lost to the darkness was eager to see that chaos reign.

"Thank you for letting me know," he replied evenly, pulling in a deep breath. "Tell the pathologists for me, tell them I said to get to work on another analysis, see if they can find something, anything, new in his blood. I'll see if we can do anything for the others."

Sam agreed with a nod and hurried away. Watching him leave, Jason couldn't help the grin that crossed his face. It was happening, and it was happening fast. He left the lab with a spring in his step, one he hoped would be mistaken for haste and urgency as he bound up the stairs to the isolation floor.

As soon as he was stuffed in a biohazard suit Jason followed the panicked flow of medical personnel. They led him to a room on the other side of the nurses' station. Just outside the door were four biohazard bins filled with bloody rags. Approaching the room, Jason peered in past the plastic curtain, seeing smears of red leading from the doorway to the back, where a pool of blood was spread. There had been an attempt to clean it judging by the swipes and swirls, but it was a fruitless effort with the body still dripping and oozing—a body yet to be removed, and even from the distance Jason could see why.

It was more than just a dead man lying on a bed. It wasn't even a man, but a...lump, was the only word he could find to describe what he saw. A lump of skin and bone no longer defining the human form. What used to be an arm was draped over the side of the bed, skin folded and hanging off bone, veins nearly purple. The stench of blood and defecation was so strong Jason could smell it even through his suit, and the smell combined with the sight of an essentially melted body nearly made him vomit.

One of the nurses wasn't as strong, and did vomit when she attempted to help lift the body onto a gurney and her hands broke through flesh, into what was left of the man's intestines. She rushed out of the room, her mask covered in her retching. Jason watched her run, then turned back to the bed to see three doctors staring at him in a line, their bird-like masks pointed straight at him.

"You don't really want to be here," one of the doctors said as he placed a sheet over the body, preparing for another attempt to move Patient Zero, all of them knowing they would likely have to take the entire mattress and burn it immediately. "They're coming in faster than we can handle, and nothing we are doing is helping control it. Whatever this virus is, it's spreading, and it's strengthening. The CDC is here to help. Let them take over and protect yourself by getting the hell out of here."

Unable to speak around the excitement welling in his chest, Jason merely nodded. He watched a few more moments before turning and heading back to the lab. On the way, he passed one of the double doors leading to the side exit. Flashes of cameras and police car lights reflected off the walls to the sound of questions and accusations being screamed at anyone who would listen.

Pausing, Jason glanced through the glass at the mass of bodies on the other side of barriers the police had apparently set up. More than just the media, he noted. Protesters with signs demanding answers, others with pictures of crosses and Christ as they prayed for the diseased. One of them, a young woman holding rosaries in both hands, caught his eye. She was saying something to the police, a prayer perhaps, but as soon as she locked eyes with Jason she quieted, going perfectly still amidst the throng.

They engaged in a silent standoff, something passing between them no one could sense, and only one of them could control. Jason felt the message slide over his skin, leave his body on a whisper, pass through a bond created with the woman outside, and enter her mind. A directive, an order, of what she must do.

The woman nodded once, blinked, then turned and slipped through the crowd.

*

It was late when Roger finally decided to call it a night and head home. He'd spent the better part of his day running interference between the hospital and media, doing his best to calm nerves, and later going over lab results to search for discrepancies. What truly infuriated him was that he couldn't find any. The results were legitimate. Baffling, but legitimate.

Still, he knew something was wrong. The Jason Waters he'd been speaking with recently was not the Jason Waters he'd known for so many years. Something was different about him, Roger just couldn't figure out what. Sure, his friend had always had a fascination will disease. They'd both watched many shows and attended even more conferences on illnesses over the decades and their effects on the populations. And yet, never had Jason been so openly...giddy about people's suffering.

He wished he could talk to Suzanne about his suspicions, but it appeared she'd managed to leave the hospital after all, judging by her unanswered phone and locked office door. If anyone could verify his concerns, it would be her. With a sigh, Roger locked up his files and shut down his computer before leaning over to grab his laptop bag from the floor.

A spot of red dripped to the floor, splashing against the pale green tile. Roger froze, staring at that spot, slowly straightening and immediately grabbing the desk when a wave of dizziness passed through him. One hand lifted to his forehead, which was hot to the touch. The other went to his nose, wet and sticky and dripping blood.

"No," he whispered, tears forming in the corners of his eyes. Resolute grief formed in the pit of his stomach. He was a doctor. He studied disease. He'd examined the sick patients.

The disease had found him.

Panic set in, panic he desperately fought to quell as he gathered his belongings, taking only one brief, depressed moment to touch the fingers of his right hand to the ring on his left, then rushed from the office as quickly as his portly body would allow. His breath came out in heaving gasps and he held his jacket to his nose to staunch the blood flow the entire elevator ride to the fifth floor.

He could see the quarantine zone from the elevator when he stepped off. Not wasting time, Roger jogged for the protection of plastic isolation, blinking past the nausea and hot flashes, past the pain in his gut, nearly choking on the blood dripping down the back of his throat. He entered the zone without hesitation, not stopping to put on a suit, ignoring the shouts from doctors and nurses already in the area.

The door had just closed behind him when Roger slumped to the floor, unconscious.

*

Sleep came easily for Jason that night, no dreams of demons or melting bodies but, rather, of beautiful women who worshiped the ground he walked upon. When he rose with the morning sun, it was with a refreshed and jovial smile. Going about his day was an almost pleasant affair. He readied himself for work with a hot shower and full breakfast at home before beginning the short drive downtown.

There was little to see this early in the day. A few cars exiting off the bridge, shop owners opening up, birds fluttering here and there. Despite the plague knocking on the city's door, most of Jacksonville's citizens had apparently turned a blind eye, choosing to pretend their lives weren't at risk, and this was just another Monday morning.

A boring Monday morning, he mused as he pulled into the hospital parking lot. And quickly saw *boring* was about to become far more interesting.

Reporters were still camped out at the front door, but they were hushed, standing in clumps and staring at something on the wall. As Jason approached, he saw what had them so fearful—a thick, red X was spray-painted over the glass doors, another over the window to the left, a third to the right…an entire row of red Xs painted alongside the wall, a menacing reminder of the death that lay inside. It was a foreboding sign, one reminiscent of days of old the symbol marked the spot of a diseased home.

Pausing, Jason looked at each X in turn, mentally counting them and thinking there were far too few for how many people would soon die. His attention then moved to the growing crowd. Cameras were starting to flash, reporters speaking into cameras as the morning news began. This was a fascinating new development for their audience and they were eager to tell the story. Eager to fan the fire and let the entire world know the St. Peters Hospital was now a breeding ground for infectious disease.

But the reporters and their frenzy-fueled words were the least of Jason's worries. He didn't care what they had to say or what their motives were for saying it. No, he cared only about one thing in this moment. There, behind all of the reporters and cameramen, stood the woman he'd sent his message to last night. She appeared haggard, her hair unbrushed, clothes wrinkled, eyes smudged with day-old makeup. Those eyes were vacant now, the soul behind driven by an unseen influence. He doubted she'd slept at all in the past twenty-four hours.

There was no time for sleep after the demon had called.

She'd been given a message, a task. Part of that task had been completed, as evidenced by the defaced hospital walls. No one could see the red paint stains on her covered arms or smell the faintest hints of aerosol in her hair, though if they looked hard enough, they'd realize the woman held a crazed look about her, one of a mind no longer in control.

In one hand she held an old-fashioned bell. Before anyone took notice of her, she moved forward a step and began ringing that bell, the sound crisp and clear and utterly out of place in the brisk morning air. Heads turned; eyes widened. Dread tightened in heart-pounding chests when the woman began calling, "Bring out your dead!"

The call was repeated, louder this time. And again, to the sound of the ringing bell, the combined sound much louder than the reporters' questions being called all around the empty-souled woman. A laugh behind Jason had him turning. On the sidewalk just outside the hospital doors he saw two men dressed in scrubs shaking their heads.

"Is she serious?" one of them asked the other.

"A bit dramatic, huh?" The second man agreed with a roll of his eyes, and both disappeared inside without a glance back at the strange scene unfolding outside their hospital.

Deciding to let their ignorance pass, Jason looked back to the woman, to the scene he had so carefully constructed in his mind. The woman walked in a circle around the reporters, ringing her bell, chanting her chant, oblivious to the questions being shouted at her, the cameras flashing in her face.

Around and around she walked, with each pass the crowd quieting a little bit more, until finally security came to escort her off the property. She went willingly and with a smile, because she knew her duty had been fulfilled, and her influence, or the influence of the one who held a grip over her mind and soul, had spread.

And, in its ever-so-carefully constructed plan, it had spread to the ones with the most *influence* over the people.

Only when the raggedy woman had disappeared from view did Jason finally turn away. The reporters still stood in their cluster, only their looks were more solemn now, more foreboding as they prepared to reveal what had just happened. When they spoke next, their words would be filled with warning, a threat of what was soon to come to the great city of Jacksonville.

Pleased with his efforts, Jason headed inside, not bothering to stop at the lab. The CDC had set up camp there, invading his space and treating him with suspicion, as though he'd been the one to cause so much sickness and suffering.

They will never know just how right they are, he told himself with a mental pat on the back. Let them be suspicious. They'd never find anything incriminating. He wouldn't let them. The demon wouldn't let them.

Bypassing his lab, Jason walked slowly through the halls, between walls fading in and out of vision, replaced by scenes of old—fires burning, people running for safety with rags over their noses, a horrible stench of death and tar. It felt as though he'd been here before, had personally witnessed the devastation brought to these people.

It was beautiful, the Asag informed him, its presence swimming through his mind to unveil snippets of the past. Jason saw the horror caused by evil. The streets of Savannah overrun with blood and bodies, gunshots ringing out in the distance as people fought to protect themselves, rodent carcasses being burned by the thousands in an attempt to clean the ports.

But all beauty fades, the demon said on a sigh. People died, but others got better. Sanitation efforts were implemented, and made a difference. The Asag could have devastated them all in one fell swoop of sickness, but chose to free these people from the clutches of its plague, and moved on.

Now, Jacksonville residents suffered the same fate, until the Asag decided to let them go.

When Jason finally made it to the isolation ward, he dressed quickly in the white biohazard suit and entered—and immediately stopped. The entire floor as far as he could see was overloaded with patients, bed upon bed lined up with only thin curtains to separate them. Even more patients were in the hall on stretchers, kept as comfortable as possible amidst the bustle around them.

Last count Jason had heard was sixty-two patients. Now there were two hundred, at least. Soon there would be nowhere to put any new arrivals. He couldn't believe how fast the number had grown, quite literally overnight, and he was only seeing the patients brought to St. Peters. There was no telling how many more were admitted to the surrounding hospitals.

Something tugged at his heart, a strange feeling of hesitation and regret. It was as though a part of himself, shoved deep into the back of his mind, had resurfaced, seeing clearly the destruction he had caused to these people. He'd always been fascinated by how quickly the healthy could fall, how fast disease could spread, yet seeing it now in a bloody cocoon of disease, it was all too much.

Doubt is for the weak.

But Jason ignored the voice whispering across his mind. His eyes had caught a horrible sight and his feet followed until he stood next to a bed occupied by one of his old college friends. Up close, he was surprised he recognized the man, who had lost a significant amount of weight. Eric appeared to be sleeping, but stirred when Jason reached out and touched his arm, unsure if he was real or an illusion.

"Jason?"

Blinking a few times, Jason realized his friend had woken up and was staring up at him. Eric's blue eyes were tinted yellow, as was his skin, now spongey and sunken. He'd even lost some of his hair, his scalp showing through in blood-crusted patches. "Eric...I didn't know you'd been admitted."

"...Whole family," the ill man replied around a curdling cough. Blood bubbled at the corners of his mouth. Gently, Jason wiped it away with gauze at his bedside. "Jason...what's wrong with us?"

"We are trying to find out," was his reply, dishonest yet heartfelt.

"This...worse ever felt."

"I know," Jason replied softly. *I built it this way.*

"...Hurts."

"I know," he said again. And it hurt him, too, to see the man in so much pain, unable to imagine what it must feel like to have one's organs slowly liquefying inside the body. Perhaps something like having a demon-possessed woman slice open his gut. "I will find a way to fix this, Eric. I will find a cure."

There is no cure for the plague to wipe away the scum.

For the first time, the gravelly voice angered him. Jason pushed against it and squeezed Eric's shoulder. "I'll figure this out, Eric. I promise."

"You have to," was the weak, raspy response from a likely dying man. Eric's hand lifted slightly, pointing. "My boys."

Looking over his shoulder, Jason saw two beds pushed close to one another, children upon them sleeping fitfully. Their expressions were pained in sleep, lips pursed and brows furrowed. Such innocence in those expressions, not understanding what was happening, utterly alone in their agony despite the hundreds of sick around them. A father unable to comfort his children, a mother two beds over unable to reach out and wrap them in warm hugs. An entire family brought to its knees.

The regret in his heart grew as he glanced back to the boys' father. "I will, Eric. You have my word." Not able to bear the sight any longer, Jason detached himself from the bedside and hurried through the ward.

Not so fast, Jason Waters, the Asag commanded. *Look. Witness. Another victim, just for you.*

The voice made him pause before he reached the door. Of its own volition, Jason's head turned and he saw a bulky frame on a bed in the corner. He recognized the man even from a distance. "Roger," he breathed, not moving to his old friend, yet not moving away either. "What have you done?"

Only what you have always desired, the Asag answered the question directed inward. *Only what the darkest parts of your heart crave.*

What frightened Jason most was that he knew the demon was right.

CHAPTER 21

News spread quickly that week, reports breaking into regularly scheduled programs to provide updates on the mystery illness. The word *plague* passed from reporters' lips to citizens' ears, only to be whispered and shouted as panic ensued.

The mayor made her appearance on a televised press conference alongside CDC experts, assuring everyone they were all perfectly safe, lying that medical progress was being made and treatments were being tested, informing them the virus was traced back to that fateful football game and asking anyone who was present to be mindful of their health and immediately visit a hospital at the first signs of illness. The CDC stepped up next, offering advice on how to stay safe and protect selves and loved ones. All the while, everyone on screen reminded residents to remain calm.

But it was too late for the CDC's speech of safety, the mayor's plea for peace. The media had already fueled the fire, reporters with blank eyes reciting demon-scripted warnings that somehow made their way into their heads, showing off red X marks painted over the doorways of the sick patients, some almost gleeful in their reports of protests and even suggesting the protests were necessary to hasten the development of a cure. Later, they wouldn't remember making such claims and showing such scenes, but for now their purpose was served.

Jason listened to all news stations as he drove home from work, then later from the safety of his living room. Almost every channel was focused on the outbreak in some form, most accusing

St. Peters for being the breeding ground of disease and failing to follow protocol. Their accusations were unfounded, but the truth no longer mattered. What did matter was that, now, more than four hundred people were sick, thirty-nine had died, and every hospital was overflowing with patients in quarantine.

Jason hadn't heard those latest stats and wondered where the media got them. He believed them, but the fact that he hadn't kept up on how many people were now sick with RYF-2 was alarming to him. Just a couple months ago he would have been running those stats himself and working day and night to make sure that number didn't grow. Now, he was barely aware of any deaths, focused only on what happened when they were sick.

"How did it get this far?" he asked himself, leaning forward on the couch and holding his head in his hands. No answer came whispering in his head, which surprised him. The demon was always willing to instill doubt, fear, and guilt in response to his questions.

Demon. The word echoed through his mind, a harsh reminder of what he'd allow happen to himself. Worse, he'd welcomed it, and for what? So people wouldn't look at him like an invalid anymore. So drunken rednecks couldn't push him around and knock him to the sidewalk. So he could have his moment of glory and finally witness firsthand what it was like when sickness ran rampant.

"I don't want it to go any farther." This he said with intention, and received the response he expected—a sharp tugging behind his eyes as the darkness thriving inside him struggled for control. Jason knew this feeling, had felt it ever since arriving home after his venture through the Savannah house, and knew how to fight it. The process was physical as much as it was mental, refusing to give up control while simultaneously accepting he never really had it in the first place.

His head began to ache. Talons of pain clenched at his consciousness, not from the Asag's own hand, but from the struggle between two souls fighting for the upper hand in one body. He was just a man, and just a man was not strong enough to hold off the darkness forever. Soon, Jason feared, he would lose the battle, unless he could find a way to either defeat the demon… or learn to live with it.

At the amended thought, Jason felt the pain behind his eyes lesson, though only a fraction. It was enough to get him off the couch and to his bedroom. He couldn't handle the news anymore and needed to sleep it away. Maybe, just tonight, he could pretend this was all a nightmare and the morning would bring with it a bright day and empty hospital.

With a sigh, Jason opened the medicine cabinet and pulled out a bottle he hadn't look at in a couple weeks; hadn't *needed* to look at, let alone use. He popped the top and dumped two pills into his palm. Sleep was desperately needed, and it would hopefully be a dreamless sleep. He needed that, craved it.

He didn't get it.

His eyes opened to a place he'd seen only once before—a desolate land with an angry river filled with floating silver bodies, trees rotted and flaky, grass wilted beneath his feet. This time, though, his walk was purposeful. Though he didn't want to be there, he at least knew what to expect, and so from the moment of his arrival Jason didn't stop moving until he'd reached the spot the demon had last appeared to him.

The wait wasn't long. All too soon the ground shook and cracked, and from it appeared the monster who called himself the Asag, the bringer of plague and sickness. Standing at full height, the two engaged in a silent standoff, one furious and just a little scared, the other curious and just a little amused. But the demon could see just how determined the human was, so it relented, just this one.

"You have come to talk," it rasped, taking a precarious step closer. "You have come for answers."

Steeling his resolve, Jason spat out, "I didn't want to come at all. I wanted to sleep and forget all about this for a few hours. But since I'm here…Yes, I want answers. I don't want to talk. I just want to know how to change what I've done, and I want my freedom."

Now the Asag reacted, one of its many brows lifting as its rocky body surged forward until they were mere inches apart. Hot breath rolled over Jason's skin, but he refused to step back. "Freedom," the creature repeated, drawing out the word, shifting and moving like a curtain of stone before the mortal man.

A hard foot kicked out, connecting with Jason's steady leg. "Where is your cane?"

A hand lifted, talon-like nail ripping the man's shirt in half. "Where are your scars?"

The Asag touched a finger to Jason's stomach, pushing inward. "Where, Jason Waters, is your pain?"

Jason swallowed hard, knowing what the demon was insinuating and refusing to answer. The beast answered for him. "I have given you freedom. I have taken from you that which made you miserable, and given you that which you have most desired."

"No," he replied, finding his voice. "I never desired this. I never desired killing hundreds of people."

"Oh, but you did. It is how I won the bid."

The bid, Jason repeated to himself. Tessa had mentioned a bidding war for souls and granted him a vision of the Will O'Wisp, but then skipped town without sticking around to explain what the hell it was he just saw. Though he hadn't understood her at the time and honestly ignored that part of her visit, the words came crashing back to him now.

"I…What bid?"

The Asag smiled its gruesome smile. "The bid for your dark, delicious soul." It edged closer still. "I am the demon of plague and disease, the keeper of the ill, the bringer of fever and death. Only the soul that longs for the feverish flesh and stench of decay can call to my own. Such a bid could not be won unless the darkest parts of your very being wanted the devastation I have brought."

One rock-hard hand touched Jason's forehead, and in a flash he observed the bid that lost him his soul.

He saw himself, creeping in a basement window, limping slowly up a set of stairs and chastising the complaining man behind him. He watched from an ethereal body as his other self stalked through the abandoned Savannah house with an almost furious stomp, desperately seeking for a clue, any clue, as to why Tessa had become what she was.

Then he witnessed the moment previously lost to him.

A dark, lanky figure emerged from a black hallway to the left of Jason, lit by the four flames burning at its fingertips. Silent in its presence, the spirit beckoned with the fiery hand, luring the pain-ridden man closer as shadows closed around him. A perfect cloak to what would soon be a sinister deed.

From his dream-state vantage point, Jason could see himself standing perfectly still, eyes staring at the wall, and yet at nothing at all. A trance brought upon by a spirit bound by evil, locking the unfortunate man in an unknown existence caused by his own curiosity and need for knowledge.

In that trance, his body seemed to light up from the inside out as four flames filled him at once, the fire flowing from the figure's fingertip straight into Jason's beating heart. In his head he counted—eight minutes the four flames consumed him, sliding through his veins as though searching for something before one of them darted out.

Three lights were left, the fire bright in his chest and head, only to have another slip out just as quickly as it came. For a long moment there was an inferno burning within him, but then a third flame disappeared as well, leaving just one behind. It searched his body, lingering in his chest, eventually taking root there instead of exiting like the others. With a quick and blinding flash, it simply faded within its new host to the sound of the man's gasp of anticipation.

"I won the bid," the Asag said again, cutting into the vision and removing his hand so it all faded away. Blinking rapidly, Jason was almost disappointed to find himself back in the wasteland, part of him wanting to see more of the bidding process. "I found the dark pieces of your soul, and I consumed them whole. Look at them, Jason Waters. Look at the dark pieces."

A wave of the demon's stone arm brought with it bodies littering the barren earth. So many bodies ripe with decay, and his ghost-like form filtering between them, sometimes pausing for a quick exam, other times chuckling over cries for help. There was no regret, no shame. Only satisfaction and a sick amount of perverse pleasure.

A choked sob escaped Jason, a realization of what he always was. The Asag laughed. "You see, now. You see how we will have such fun."

His head clouded when the demon smiled, even as he fought for control. Confusing him more was when the Asag added, "Do you know how I knew you were the one, Jason Waters? How I knew I'd made the right choice?" Refusing to answer, Jason merely clamped his jaw shut, staring through teary eyes at the illusion of bodies before him. The Asag pressed himself against the mortal soul.

"You never feared me, my presence, like any normal human would do." One hand tapped Jason's temple, a reminder of the influence thriving there.

"You never questioned my desires, my affections for the taste of blood and rot." A tap to his heart, memories of the pleasure taken in creating a deadly virus.

"You welcomed my touch upon your skin, craved the lust your body was granted." Hard fingers grazed up his arms, a suggestion of the fantasies he'd indulged in.

"I…No. No!" Jason shook himself free and stepped back.

"Just because there is some part of me that likes it, I never wanted it to go this far. You...you're just trying to distort the truth."

"The truth?" An arm lashed out, and Jason felt a slice of pain in his stomach. The other arm, causing more agony that had the man falling to his knees. "Your life was stripped from you the moment Tessa Taylor stepped into that house. *That* is your truth. And now you will spend your life in suffering, each year worse than the other. You will die in your prime, your injuries too severe to last you a long lifetime."

When Jason's eyes widened, the demon grinned again. "Ah, and so the *truth* shall set you free."

The jaw clamped in his gut was too much to bear. It turned him into the invalid, the cripple, the pathetic cretin who could do nothing but complain about the shitty hand life had dealt him. It didn't matter who caused it, whose fault it was. What did matter was he knew he couldn't be this person. He wasn't *meant* to be this person.

"Stop," he found himself pleading before he really knew what he was asking. "I don't want to live like this. But I don't want to lose myself like Tessa did. You'll have to kill me before I let you do that to me."

The burning sensation lessened as the Asag considered his words. Bouldered shoulders rose and fell with heavy breaths of excitement. "Coexist," it murmured, both a consideration and a tease. "Perhaps you are worthy after all. I will take from you your knowledge, your life as you know it, your hopes and dreams and beliefs."

Finally able to catch his breath, Jason pushed himself to his feet and tried to face the demon squarely. If he was going to go out—without fear, as he'd done all along—then it would be on his terms. "And what do I get in return?"

The stabbing sensation in his stomach disappeared, a pointed reminder of how quickly his entire life could change with the help—or hindrance—of a demon.

"You take from me my power," that demon rasped in his ear, Jason's body strengthening with each syllable. He felt stronger, invincible.

"You take from me my influence over the world." He saw the potential future flash before his eyes—Jason awarded metals of commendation for his medical breakthroughs, hailed a hero for saving the people of the city, of the country, of the world.

"You take from me the fever of the darkness." Stoney skin melted into creamy flesh, a bulky frame into slender curves, until standing before him was a perfect specimen of red-headed seductress.

"Clara," Jason breathed, his body immediately tightening as his mind spun. Even knowing who—what—she was, he still found his eyes roving over her naked form, locking on her mouth when she licked her lips in anticipation. The need to have and control her was nearly overwhelming. He didn't understand where those feelings came from, and yet he didn't want to know, so long as she kept looking at him like that and making his body respond the way it did with just a bat of her beautifully green eyes.

Two eyes, he managed to think around the fog of lust. Not dozens, like the beast that stood before him only seconds ago. The thought roused him enough to say, "You...you're just an illusion."

In response, Clara merely smiled. She took a few steps closer until her bare breasts brushed against his chest. One hand slipped over his shoulders, a soft finger stroking down his cheek. "What is life, Jason, but an illusion? Love. Lust. Happiness. Misery. All is an illusion, unless you believe it to be real."

Her other hand dropped lower to massage him, and her grin widened when she felt him harden. "I have had you, Jason Waters. I have tasted you. You have felt my body around yours. Was it not real?"

He wanted to say no, wanted to believe he hadn't been tempted by a demon in disguise. But he knew it would be a lie. He had been tempted...and he had enjoyed it. Worse, he wanted more.

"You can have me," she purred in his ear, fingers working at his zipper, sliding inside to grasp him, hard and ready. "Every day, every night, I will be yours, if you want me."

His mind clouded, a haze of heated desire blinding him. Yet he didn't fight through it. This feeling, this power he had over a woman who would be entirely his, was what he craved most of all in this moment. The feel of her soft hands stroking him, the hardened peaks of her breasts rubbing against him, lush red lips forming a perfect pout—the woman who thought she would own him would, instead, *be* owned.

Eyes opening to find hers already searching his face, Jason gripped the back of her neck, hand tangling in her hair as he bared her throat to him. "I want this. I want you. Now."

He moved to kiss her, but Clara stopped him with a hand to his chest, the other still wrapped around his cock. "If you want me," her tongue traced up his neck, along his jaw, "then you must call me."

Both puzzled and annoyed, Jason tightened his grip, forcing her closer. "Call you what?" The reply was coarse, unforgiving. And when she only smiled up at him, he remembered his first meeting with the Asag.

You will be my greatest servant, and you will call me master.

"Never," Jason snarled, his grasp so tight on Clara's neck she whimpered in his clutches.

"You will," she said around her pain, smiling despite the fingers digging into her flesh. "Or I will take everything from you."

Everything. Power that took away his crippling scars. The ability to create a deadly virus. A future where his name was celebrated, not talking about in news reports as a murderer's first victim.

Everything was too much. He couldn't afford to lose it all and gain nothing in return.

It was nearly painful to form the single word that would set him free. Jason jerked her head back, staring down into those seductive eyes, instantly lost in swirls of green, forgetting his problems with her every stroke, every lick of ruby-red lips.

"Master," came the word she sought. "I call you master."

His lips lowered to her throat; Clara's own eyes closed and her hand began to work him. In his ecstasy he didn't notice the heat that befell them, wrapping the duo in a cocoon of power and union. Nor did he care what may happen, who may see, whether this was a dream or reality—all he cared about was taking her for himself and making this moment his, and no one else's.

Fever was like that, all consuming and selfish, able to be cured only by the remedy made just for it. And, right now, Clara was his cure.

Capturing her mouth, Jason kissed her deeply, fingers tangling in her red hair as his other arm wrapped around her waist as he lowered them both to the hard, unforgiving ground. Her legs wrapped around his waist and he covered her body with his own, hips grinding against each other. The heat grew, a humid breeze brushing against fevered flesh, the river bubbling and thrashing in wild waves to the rhythm of his lips moving down her throat, tongue tracing across her breasts, mouth biting a path down until he was tasting her.

Clara moaned his name, thin hands in his hair, hips lifting as his tongue entered her, only to be replaced by his fingers when his mouth returned to her center and sucked at the tender flesh. His cock strained against his pants as he continued to work her until her entire body was quivering and she was begging for release.

He gave her that release, hooking and sliding his fingers in and out as his tongue licked at her. When her body fell limp with a hard-beating heart, Jason rose to his knees and took a moment to observe the beauty before him. Her skin was slick with sweat, chest heaving, hands massaging her breasts—a woman thoroughly and wholly pleased.

He wanted her on her knees.

A growl rumbled in his throat. Jason pulled Clara from the

ground and spun her around, positioning her. Knowing what he desired, she moved to her hands and knees, pressing herself against him as he freed himself. No time was spent on loving words; he entered her from behind in one firm thrust.

"Jason, wait," she gasped when he was seated fully inside. He grasped her hips, both their bodies stilling, though his fingers tightened on her waist as he strained against the desire to move.

"Jason," she said again, the sound of his name on her lips intoxicating. "You must do something for me, before we continue, to prove your loyalty to our coexistence."

When her hips rocked ever so slightly, Jason grit his teeth together, his cock throbbing within her with a nearly uncontrollable need to thrust. In this moment he would have done anything she asked if it meant feeling himself pump inside her heated folds.

"What?" he ground out the word, dragging his hand down her slender back, cherishing her soft flesh.

Moving her hips in small circles, Clara reached back and took his hand, wrapping it around her and placing his fingers against her center. Both moaned in unison. "You must protect me from the one who seeks to take me from you." She gasped when he began working her.

"No one will take you from me," he snarled, possession clear in his tone. To stake his claim he began to move with her, harder and faster, grabbing hold of her long hair with one hand as the other stroked her into oblivion.

"You must kill the one who wants to destroy me." Clara's legs spread farther as he thrust into her, her body spasming around him, wet and warm and demanding more.

More he was willing to give. More he demanded to give. "Name him," Jason commanded on a grunt, ready to pump faster, harder.

Pleasure growled from her lips as she whispered just seconds before his hot release inside her, "You must kill Roger Willcox."

CHAPTER 22

The time for basking in the glory of the unknown had come to an end. When Jason awoke the next morning, refreshed, without doubt, and his mind entirely his own for the foreseeable future, he was ready to give the world a name to the disease it now feared. Memories of a night spent with Clara made him grin a lascivious grin, already lusting for another round with the woman who would only ever be his. He could still feel her hands stroking him, her hot center massaging him. Never again would he need anything more than to simply think her name.

Self-assurance and a newfound arrogance followed him to work, directed him through the movements in his lab. He'd brought with him the materials needed to feign a sudden revelation—blood samples and tests he'd already run, now appearing as though he'd just discovered their results. Tina Burns was stationed at her new desk in his lab and kept a close eye on him, but she was just a woman, susceptible to the darkness' influence like the others, and her eyes turned away from his activities whenever ordered to do so.

The spy sent to watch, reduced to nothing more than a prop in his war.

Once his ruse was set up and he was ready, Jason printed the results and organized his files, then took a moment to himself. As soon as he left this lab, it would be over. All his hard work would be but a blip in the history books. The file in his hands would mark the beginning of the end to his reign. He'd enjoyed being the only one who knew what ailed these people.

But, he reminded himself, soon he would enjoy something even greater—the city groveling at his feet when he cured them.

Up ten flights, he reached the executive suite on the top floor of the hospital. He knocked lightly on the director's door before entering. Gary glanced up from his phone call, eyes narrowing. Jason merely pushed forward and dropped the file on the man's desk. "You need to see this."

Gary leafed through the file, his expression quickly changing from hesitant to urgent. "I'll call you back," the director said to the person on the other end, then hung up and stood. "Is this what I think it is?"

"Confirmed results for RYF-2." Jason nodded, keeping his face neutral when he really wanted to grin.

Frowning, Gary pressed two fingers to each temple and stared down at the papers. "RYF-2?"

"Resurrected Yellow Fever, the number two for the new virus strand." Noticing the expression on the director's face, Jason shrugged. "What do you expect? I test blood samples. I don't spend my days coming up with good disease names."

"I don't care what it's called so long as we have a name for it. Tell me about this virus."

Pleased that his name wouldn't be changed, Jason said, "RYF-2 has its roots in yellow fever, but it's not the same virus, which is why we were hitting so many roadblocks in the beginning. It's mutated. It mutated long before it ever reached our patients, if my guesses are correct. We're looking at a different strain of yellow fever, much like you have various strains of the flu, hepatitis, HPV, et cetera. This is, for all intents and purposes, a brand-new virus."

The breath escaped Gary in a long sigh. "How is this possible? I don't even remember the last time there's been a case of yellow fever in the US, let alone Jacksonville. None of our patients, Keven Carlson included, have traveled out of the US recently or done anything that would explain a sudden exposure. How could the yellow fever virus have not only found a host, but also mutated, in so short a time?"

Anything is possible with the power of darkness, Jason thought, but instead he said, "That information is there, further down the page. I believe this can be traced back to Savannah, a specific site, and a specific person." He waited until the director read his notes through unblinking eyes.

"Are you saying…" His voice trailed off the more he read, not wanting to believe what was suggested on the page. His scientific mind wasn't able to process the proposal. "How would that even be possible?"

"I don't know how it's possible," Jason answered easily. "It may even be a crazy, unfounded theory. But it's the best I've got right now. Though, Gary, trying to figure out how the impossible just became possible right now would take time we don't have. Right now, we have to focus on treatment."

"Treatment?" Gary dropped the file and shook his head. There was a cloud of confusion slowing him down as he desperately tried to understand. "There is no treatment for yellow fever, only the symptoms. And how can we treat a virus that mutated like this? Can you find a cure for this?"

"I will. I won't let you down. Get those results to the CDC and see what they think. That Burns woman is in there now, but I wanted to show this to you first. We'll see what they think, then go from there."

Leaving the file for the director, Jason headed for the door, stopped only when Gary said after him, "Dr. Willcox, he mentioned yellow fever and ordered these workups in the very beginning. I figured he was just grasping at straws and didn't think anything of it at the time. Now, though…It's like he knew something we didn't."

A hollow pit ached inside Jason, cold and brutal. Slowly that pit began to fill with rage, a fury no mortal could ever know, all-consuming in its otherworldly power. "Perhaps he did, and karma is now at work."

*

A promise had been made to find a cure, and now a promise had to be kept to eliminate the enemy.

Jason felt the demon inside fighting for control. This time, he gave himself over without fight, and allowed his consciousness to slip away into the background, unable to lead but aware of everything.

His skin warmed as the Asag took control. His heart beat slower, breaths lengthened. Living was almost a laborious affair, and yet peaceful, purposeful. Jason let the demon lead him down to the fifth floor. He passed nurses, doctors, janitorial staff—they all slowed in his presence, time itself affected by his very being. By the time he reached the quarantine zone, there was little activity, and even less noise.

He entered the ward, wasting no time heading to Roger's bedside, sliding the thin curtain closed for privacy—not that it was needed. There was no one around to witness what would soon be done. A glance up at the cameras in the room, and he knew there would be no evidence. His power was too great, his influence too strong. Even as he lived and breathed in this body, those on the other side of the cameras were destroying footage of his presence.

His dark influence was a beautiful thing.

Jason scraped a chair closer to the bed, nearly salivating at the excitement of being so in control of this body and mind, to finally have the chance to speak. One hand rested on the mattress next to Roger's arm. Roger, having woken up at the raucous sound in such silence, tried to move his limb away, but was too weak, and settled for a whimper. Jason smiled, and when he spoke, it was with a voice not his own, yet so very similar that the ailing man wondered if he was hallucinating the whole thing.

"I've seen this before," Jason said quietly, glancing around the room with that eerie smile still on his face. "In a place called Savannah, not so far back, in the 1800s." Roger made a sound at that, not able to speak but the panic clear in his eyes. "Oh, you know this story? Well...did you know that *I* brought death to those people?"

He shifted in the hard plastic chair, excitement lighting up his eyes. "I brought it to them. They thought mosquitos had carried with them a plague like the city had never known before. But no, *I* set the city on fire with a sickness that spread from that dirty, rat-infested port and through their streets in a flood of fever and blood. Just two weeks." He held up two fingers in front of his face. "Two weeks to take the lives of more than one thousand bodies. One thousand, Roger. Can you imagine it?"

With a chuckle, Jason sat back and watched Roger for a moment. His face was gaunt and pale, a shadow of the portly doctor he'd once been. In just a few short days his weight had dropped dramatically. Pain was evident in the wince etched into his expression. But Jason hardly took notice of this. His attention was on the slow beat of the doctor's heart, the heat that radiated from his flesh, the smell of disease in his veins.

"They fled by the thousands, Roger," he continued, once more lowering his face to the other man. "Friends turned enemy as they ran over one another to flee from the terrifying sickness that plagued their beloved city. And the doctors. The doctors!" He laughed, but it was a dark, unfeeling laugh. "Their patients came to them in pain. Fevers, body pains, skin turning so yellow it was almost green, and the blood, so much blood pouring from their bodies."

Jason touched a finger to one of the bandages tucked under Roger's ear, where dried blood formed a path down the side of his neck. "The doctors blamed the swamps, the mosquitos, a tropical illness that fell with the heavy summer rains and rose with the temperatures. You doctors, always trying so hard to explain away the unexplainable with *science*."

Roger swallowed hard and tried to turn his head, turn away from the man who had once been such a good friend, now a stranger spouting nonsense. But, he feared it wasn't really nonsense, and that, perhaps, Jason was trying to tell him something. So he listened, even as he feared the man in front of him wasn't really a man at all.

"An epidemic, they called it." Jason waved a hand dramatically while rolling his eyes. "A plague brought on by the tiniest of winged and tailed beasts. A blood virus that suffocated the most vital organs. Panic plagued the city just as heavily as the sickness that I gifted it with. And yes, it was such a gift." He rubbed his hands together. "Their bodies burning. Blood crusting on their pale skin. Their stomachs so full of blood that their vomit stuck to their throats. And it was beautiful."

Somehow, Roger saw the past—the words Jason spoke forming a scene inside his mind. So much suffering, families torn apart by disease, a city torn in half by fear and chaos. Faces wrapped in homemade masks, roads coated in dried blood, bodies piled up in preparation for burial in mass graves. Crying, all day and night, wails and sobs over the deceased. Promises to find a cure, even as desolation overshadowed hope.

"Eventually, it stopped being fun," Jason sighed as the vision floated away. "There is only so much entertainment in death. Cities must rebuild. People must procreate. After all, if everyone is dead, who is there to infect? And so I let them live. Oh, they cleaned up their swampy city so the insects couldn't breed and believed in better hygiene, thinking they had taking precautions. Your entire country thought it had learned from one city's mistake. But," Jason said, wicked glee in his voice, "the true mistake was in believing it was ever healed at all."

"Do you know what will happen next?" he continued, one

finger tracing up the tube that led to Roger's nose. "History will repeat itself, as it always does. Your doctors will find something to blame, some *science*. Your doctors will ask for charity, for *awareness*, for help as they exhaust their resources trying to save this city. And then those charities will be exhausted as well as panic spreads and your entire nation begins to feel the fear of disease coming to their city. Already you see red Xs painted at the thresholds of homes. Soon, corpses will be left on the streets to be thrown in mass graves. And your precious physicians, the pillars of your society, will run themselves into devastation as the public turns on them and blames *them* for such death." Jason took in a deep breath, releasing it slowly as his eyes closed to relish the sensation his next words wrought deep in his belly.

"And I will laugh as they cry."

A rough scoff sounded from Roger's throat, drawing Jason's eyes to meet his. "Who...?"

"Who am I?" he finished for the man too weak to complete a sentence. "I am the one you called friend, the one you turned against when you were needed most of all. Did you know," Jason held up a hand in a mocking gesture, "your friend is no longer in control of his soul?"

The virus-infected man's sallow eyes widened, then narrowed in confusion. Eager to reveal the truth, Jason added, "I found him, lost in the dark of a Savannah home. I found him, and I took him, and now we have brought the plague of the past to your great city."

He read the doubt and disdain in Roger's expression. Jason's mood visibility shifted, the smirk of pleasure and entertainment fading into barely concealed rage. "The sailors died first, then I took the rest," he said, leaning in close so his next words were spoken into one blood-crusted ear. "And now I will take you."

Leaning back, Jason reached into his coat pocket and produced a single glass tube filled with a black substance. Roger's teary eyes followed the move, the rest of him unable to move, though his body started to quake in terror when that black liquid began to bubble, impossibly heated to a boiling point in Jason's hand.

The hot vial moved closer, touching his mouth. Roger pressed his lips together and refused entry. Not to be deterred, Jason stood and took hold of the doctor's jaw.

"Rejoice," Jason said quietly, his fingers prying open the sick man's mouth. "You are a doctor, experiencing the old ways of healing by your brethren. Witness how far you have come, as you move toward your end."

The tube tipped upward, black tar rolling across the glass, dripping into Roger's open mouth. Lips seared at first contact, tongue blistered as bitter, boiling blackness slid across. His body convulsed, the tar sticking in his throat, choking and burning.

Jason placed the vial in his pocket with one hand and held the other over Roger's mouth. Forcing the doctor to swallow, reveling in the aroma of a body on fire from the inside out. "You suspected yellow fever," he said down to Roger, whose eyes were wide, blood-coated tears cascading from the corners. "You wanted this disease, good doctor. Do you not want to be treated?"

An inhuman strength kept Roger's bucking body from falling off the bed. But it did not stop the blisters from popping in his mouth, the skin that peeled back from muscle and tendon in his throat, the holes expanding in his stomach as the tar melted against it. A gurgled cry bubbled out around Jason's fingers and then the doctor was still and silent, save for the faint hiss of tar against flesh.

Satisfied, Jason wiped his hands on the sheet and stared down at the man's unmoving form, disappointed by the lack of fight. "Weak," he muttered, then took a deep breath, allowing time to right itself once more. Dimmed lights flickered back to full power, machines beeped, the monitor at Roger's bedside erupting in one long wail. Jason was pushed out of the way as nurses and doctors rushed over, not even seeing the unmasked visitor who watched and listened.

"Doctor Willcox was one of ours," a nurse replied around her tears.

"Another one gone, a good one," a doctor commented, frustration clear in her voice. "That makes seventy-nine deaths in two days."

"Eighty." The second doctor glanced up when the others peered at him in question. "They just found Doctor Suzanne Hart in her office. They don't even know how long she's been in there because the door was locked. Someone noticed the smell. They just quarantined off that floor in the past hour, and are moving patients so they can admit more of the ones with the mystery disease. I just came up from the ICU and it's overrun with these patients because there's nowhere to put them."

The first doctor's head hung for a moment. Defeat was clear in his expression. "We need to shut this hospital down," he whispered, throwing the sheet over Roger's body. "We need to shut the whole goddamn city down."

*

Pulled out of the shadows by the chaos of the city, the Will O'Wisp conjured its mind's eye, curious of the happenings of the world. On the streets people gathered, shouting at one another, blaming their historic city for the spread of a disease infecting dozens, and killing rapidly. It filtered through visions gifted by— cursed by—its creator in this task to harbor souls of evil:

The call had been made. Jacksonville's borders were closed to all who would enter, and all who would leave. Highways were barricaded, smaller streets sectioned off, police at every possible outlet and waterways monitored. Rumors spoke of military reinforcement on the way, with local navy and Army stations already set up to protect the people, protect the city. On I-95 and I-4, traffic was at a standstill, horns blaring and frightened passengers shouting at the police, who shouted back they would not allow passage. Men and women were arrested as they fled the safety of their vehicles and attempted to skirt around the squad cars on foot. Local jails quickly filled up and resources were quickly exhausted, too many people and too few officers.

Just a few hours away, the city of Savannah found itself in quarantine as well, its borders closed all the same. Locals fretted about their safety, tourists worried how they would find their way home. CDC officials scoured old maps and documents in search of years-old graves, aided by tour guides and historians, including one Augustus Jones. A frenzy had been crafted by the media, and it was a frenzy spreading up and down the East Coast.

Every news station in Jacksonville and Savannah reported on RYF-2, the mutated form of yellow fever now being blamed on Tessa Taylor. The rumor originated in Jason's report—the perfect scapegoat for a plague that needed its villain, and its hero. Board director Gary Day perpetuated the rumor, all too happy to finally have someone to blame, a target taken off the hospital and onto the woman already wanted for murder and mayhem. And reporters were all too happy to spread the word, even if they did not realize how many of those words were inspired by the darkness influencing their hearts.

"Medical experts have spent the past two weeks searching for clues as to what caused the outbreak of this mysterious disease. As it turns out, it was not a case of *what*, but rather, *whom*," one reporter announced as part of her breaking news segment. "Doctors initially suspected yellow fever, and began an intensive study of the patients, lab results, and the disease. In the past two days, medical experts have diagnosed this as RYF-2, a mutation of yellow fever nicknamed Resurrect Fever, given that we are seeing a resurrected form of the yellow fever disease."

The reporter paused, a purely dramatic effect. "The team at St. Peters Hospital is hard at work to find a treatment and cure for Resurrect Fever. In the meantime, Jacksonville medical and city officials are working hand in hand with both the CDC and Savannah officials to determine the exact infection site and answers as to how the virus could spread."

Her expression turned even more somber. "While we do not yet know *how* it happened, we do know this much. Tessa Taylor, a former phlebotomist at St. Peters Hospital, visited Savannah with her fiancé and best friend just a couple months before her alleged breakdown last year. In Savannah, she cut her hand on a tree allegedly growing atop a mass burial site for yellow fever victims back in the late 1800s. Her boss at the time, Jason Waters, remembers her with a bandaged hand and claims of clumsiness while on a ghost tour in Savannah. You may remember Jason Waters as being Tessa Taylor's first victim."

Another pause, another dramatic expression. "Tessa Taylor and her brother, Braden, are rumored to have recently returned to Jacksonville. The Taylor Sibling Slaughters are being blamed for the murder of a local father of six just one week ago. The medical team at St. Peters Hospital now believes Tessa discovered traces of the virus in her blood after going through a routine exam upon her return from Savannah, and utilized her laboratory's resources to manufacture a mutated form of the yellow fever virus. Officials believe the Taylor siblings were in hiding in Jacksonville for at least a month, as Tessa's recent return to Jacksonville corresponds with the timeline for the first patients' falling ill, so it is believed she brought the virus back with her, perhaps to take revenge against the city that was formerly her own."

Now the reporter sat up straighter. "But there is hope. Jason Waters is back at work after recovering from Tessa's attack, and has vowed to find a cure to this horrible disease. Police, city, and CDC officials are asking that the citizens of our great city give Waters and his team the time they need to find this solution, and to remain calm and peaceful."

The Will O'Wisp sighed, knowing calm and peace would never be had. But knowing didn't mean he had to watch. Closing its eyes, the spirit hoped Jason Waters was stronger than Tessa Taylor, and would fight the darkness within.

CHAPTER 23

Despite the reporter's weakly spoken plea for peace, the Asag's influence spread, passing from words through a television, through a wary glance by a stranger, with the very passing of time. Some influence was strengthened by the demon, the rest by fear and panic alone—a powerful combination in a city already brimming with tension. Overnight, all of Jacksonville collapsed upon itself, terror reigning, sensibility in hiding.

On day three of anarchy, Jason basked in destruction brought by disease as he strolled through downtown. Somewhere four streets behind him he'd left his vehicle, unable to travel past the chaos. Mobs of people ran this way and that, some carrying stolen goods, others fighting off the vermin who had come out of hiding to take what they'd formerly been denied by law and order.

A step in the middle of a street littered with trash and abandoned cars showed him the beginnings of a ruined city. Storefronts were shattered and smudged with soot, business owners desperately boarding up windows and doors while looters stole right out from under them. Cops shouted at thieves and rioters, making arrests where they could, running for their own lives when necessary. Firemen attempted to put out flames, but their trucks were overrun and fire hydrants busted by people who'd rather watch the world burn.

A continued walk through alleys and side streets toward the hospital revealed the truth of the world—time always ran backward when panic was in charge. Men and women wrapped scarves, jackets, bags, anything they could use as masks around their mouths, only their eyes showing in a desperate attempt to protect themselves. Children clung to their parents' hands even as the temptation to run wild shone in their eyes. People set fire to dilapidated buildings, dropped fireworks and homemade explosives into the sewer, shooting and stomping the rats as they scurried to escape. Barrels filled with tar and oil burned along the sides of the roads, thick black smoke billowing up to a gray sky. An old, last-ditch attempt to rid the city of disease—an attempt that would soon prove futile.

A leisurely stroll along the waterfront reminded Jason of the great power he now held. The river roiled, turbulent and fierce, silver-scaled bodies belly-side up as they floated upon the surface. With the inky tar at his back, the scent of rotting aqua life all around, and the X-marked hospital at his front, Jason had never felt so powerful. Stopping in place, he allowed himself a moment to take it all in: black smoke rising from burning buildings, screams echoing down alleys, horns blaring, cars crashing, sirens in the distance, dead fish floating in a boiling river.

Hell had arrived, and it was glorious.

All too soon his walk came to an end, and Jason was standing at the shattered front doors of St. Peters Hospital. There were only a few reporters brave enough to keep the public updated amidst the riots, but they ignored him, focusing instead on the cameras and their own safety. It made no matter to Jason. He—the Asag—had had his moment of glory and it was now time to use the mortal's knowledge to turn chaos into hope.

"The world is yours once more," Jason said, one half of himself flickering inward, allowing the other half to emerge.

Jason, the non-demon Jason Waters, took in a deep breath, almost reluctant to take charge once more. Part of him was sad to see the madness end. "All good things must come to an end," he muttered to himself, then got to work.

Six hours later, he'd made no progress other than a massive headache. Throwing down a microscope slide across the table, Jason rubbed at his forehead, ignoring the questioning looks sent his way by the two CDC officials just outside his office. They, too, were working to find a cure, supposedly with him, sometimes against him, though he only gave what little information was necessary for progress, but not success. It was obvious they didn't trust him, despite finding no evidence of wrongdoing in his lab, and therefore kept their distance. Their cold shoulders were fine with him. Jason knew they would never find their cure. He was the only one with such knowledge, even if he hadn't yet found it within himself.

This was a disease he had easily crafted, but it wasn't one so easily cured—nor was it ever meant to be. So far, they'd been able to culture the virus from affected patients' blood, but none were forming antibodies against it yet. Antiviral medications were not effective; the antibodies were what he needed and without them, there was no immediate, possible cure.

"I need help," he admitted, speaking not to himself, but to the darkness lurking deep in the shadows of his soul.

Help was not part of the deal, Jason Waters, was the response. *You must use your knowledge, and your knowledge alone.*

Knowledge he had, but the question was, did he have the *right* knowledge? A bookshelf behind him held the answers to many of life's greater medical questions, though none of them would offer much assistance with a disease cultivated by a demon, using the blood of a possessed woman. No, this cure would require his own ingenuity.

The problem was that Jason was not a man prone to imagination and fancy. He didn't understand how people could so easily make up stories and believe in magic and think "outside the box" by using creativity to solve an equation. He dealt with facts, numbers, and truths.

"So what are the truths?" he asked himself.

Tessa Taylor was possessed by a demon after entering the Savannah house on Abercorn. He now believed that much to be true.

Tessa's blood became infected with a mutated form of yellow fever—a mutation completely separate from her possession, but enhanced by it nonetheless.

Using her tainted blood and samples of vegetation around the burial site, Jason created a brand-new virus, and used said virus to infect hundreds of people at a football game on a Sunday afternoon.

The virus was more than just an infection strengthened by years buried beneath the earth. It was strengthened by powers of the underworld.

Only the powers of the underworld could cure its own disease, except he was left to figure out an antidote on his own.

And one final truth: none of his reflections made a damn bit of difference.

"And so the demon wins again." A sigh of frustration accompanied the book he shoved off his desk. The resounding *bang* when it hit the floor jolted Jason upright.

An idea formed. A longshot, and probably ridiculous, but the only thing he could think of at the moment. Abandoning the microscope in favor of a different kind of research, he slid in his chair over to his desk, firing up the computer and impatiently waiting for the Internet to load. Quickly, he typed *the Asag* in a Google search and dove into the many links that populated. He'd done this same research before, but back then he'd only been searching for proof he wasn't losing his mind. Now he had a purpose.

He was looking for a way to defeat the Asag.

His search yielded him several Wikipedia entries, a whole host of images, lots of legends and lore. Too many names, stories, and pictures raced past his eyes, none of it making sense. He was growing more confused with each click of the mouse, and feeling more defeated every time he closed out a window. Shifting gears, he tried again, searching *how to defeat the Asag*. And there, the first result, held promise of an answer.

"Rock demon offspring accompanied the great warrior, the Asag, in a revolt against the gods," he murmured, trying to piece everything together. So the demon of plague and sickness was a soldier, a leader.

"Tasked by Nintura, god of war." A war leader trusting the demon to fight his war, to remain loyal. Then the Asag turned against the god of war, and so began a fierce battle for power, for control.

"Nintura couldn't defeat the Asag and end his reign of terror. So began the dark days, filled with sickness, as Nintura struggled to find a way to kill his new enemy." A body of stone immune to arrows and spears and daggers. The god of war desperate for a way to defeat the warrior he'd brought into the battle.

"And, finally, a weak spot in the stone armor, a battle ax that pierced the Asag's liver." The blow that brought down Goliath, ending the fight between god and demon once and for all. One strike to the beast's liver, the Achilles heel to an otherwise indestructible force.

"Gotcha," Jason whispered with a grin.

*

For seven days he worked, never leaving the lab, hardly eating, sleeping in small fits between tests, and more tests. Lab techs came to his aid when they could, but Jason felt entirely alone in his fight to save the innocent. Especially when the CDC all but laughed in his face when he proposed his solution and went back to their own efforts. Now they worked side by side in the same lab, but on very different treatment tests.

His head lifted from his hands when the office door opened and Sam stepped through. The young tech intern looked just as tired, though not nearly as despondent. "Hey, boss," he greeted as he took a seat across from Jason.

"Sam. Any news from isolation?" Jason already knew the entire floor had been warded off, along with sections of the second, seventh, and eighth where patients had fallen ill. He also knew that, in the past week while he'd been trying to develop a cure, there were now more than eight hundred patients fighting for their lives at the seven hospitals throughout Jacksonville, and just under five hundred total who had passed away.

It seemed the virus had reached its peak incubation period, and now those patients first diagnosed were rapidly dropping off, inciting greater public outcry and crippling the hospitals. Biohazard bins were overflowing with bloody rags and sheets, the incinerator running constantly to keep up with the backlog of infected materials. It was hard to see floor between the patients, and nearly impossible to fit additional bodies.

But more than space and power was the people, the staff tasked with caring for so many. They were exhausted, running on less than fumes, barely taking time to eat or sleep in order to keep up with patient care demand. The media and public blasted them for not doing enough, when the reality, behind closed doors, was they were refusing to do anything less, and all but killing themselves to be there when needed.

And, right now, they were needed every moment of every day.

"Give me good news, Sam," he added when he saw the intern's miserable expression. At this point, Jason was surprised the college student hadn't quit, and was impressed by his dedication to the hospital, and its patients.

Sam sighed and scrubbed a hand over his face. "Half the nursing staff has quit or gotten sick. The remaining doctors who aren't sick are being run ragged trying to keep up. At this point they are even allowing volunteers to help with the patients, though most of their jobs are cleaning up and making way for new sick people. I heard someone say that by the end of the week, they probably won't have enough people to care for every patient every day. That's just here. I don't know what's happening at the other hospitals."

When his boss closed his eyes and shook his head, Sam decided not to speak of the red-stained footprints lining the tile throughout the isolation zone, or the bodies being stacked up in the morgue and hallway just outside its door, nowhere to put them. Instead he asked, "How is the treatment coming?"

At the question, Jason laughed. "Coming? It's not coming. It's not fucking working."

"Tell me." When Jason glanced up, confused, Sam clarified, "Tell me about what you're doing. I may not understand it all, but maybe talking it through with someone will help."

What the hell, Jason figured, and placed a stack of papers in front of Sam covered in charts and diagrams, then placed a 3D model of a liver on top of them. "I'm trying to create not only a treatment, but a cure. So, how do we do that?" He pointed to one of the diagrams. "We isolate an antibody to fight the disease. The problem? There *isn't* an antibody. So I'm trying to manufacture a new one, in a sense."

Sam knew as much, and had helped his boss work through some of the formulas over the past few days. "Okay, so where does the liver come into play?"

Everywhere, if I'm smart enough to figure it out.

"I had an idea," Jason replied over his thoughts and picked up the model. "Probably a stupid one, but I figure, innovation comes from crazy ideas, right? So…what does the liver do? It creates proteins the body has to have to survive, proteins that help blood clot so we don't bleed out. What's happening to our patients? They are bleeding out internally and externally and *never* clotting. Why not?"

Before Sam could venture a guess, Jason rushed on. "The liver also produces bile so we can absorb our food and push toxins out of our body. Without bile, or when the flow of bile is obstructed due to liver failure, patients began to become jaundiced. Coincidence?"

There was only one answer, but Jason didn't give the younger man a chance to answer. "And finally, the liver filters poisons out of the blood. What is a virus but a poison the body can't rid itself of? The liver's entire job is to detoxify the blood. It's essentially the body's cleaning crew when it comes to blood. You need the liver to fight off infection."

He opened the 3D model and gestured to the various components inside. "To that end, it also recycles hemoglobin when red blood cells die. Our patients are losing blood by the pint, which makes them anemic, which means their red blood cell counts are dangerously low."

His stare penetrated Sam, who shook his head. "Okay. I get what the liver does and how it relates to what our patients are going through. But, what's the point? I don't mean to be rude. I am just having trouble seeing where this is going."

The words flowed from lips curling into a small smile. "What if we could find a way to isolate and harvest the Hgb molecule, attach a cure to it, and transfuse them?"

Excitement shone in Jason's blue eyes, even through the exhaustion. Sam could see the older man truly believed what he said was possible. And, Sam considered while chewing on his bottom lip, who was he to say it couldn't be done?

"How are you going to attach a cure to the Hgb molecule?"

"I don't know," Jason admitted. "That's where I'm stuck. The theory is there, but not the execution. Every test I've run doesn't affect the virus at all. If anything, the virus just consumes it. I tried getting some insight from the CDC, but they just rolled their eyes at me. But this, this is it. I know it is. I just need to figure out what I'm missing."

Sitting back, Sam took a moment to reflect. He wasn't the best at coming up with treatments, and would much rather skip out on a day of work to play video games than read a medical book. This virus had changed that outlook some, seeing all the doctors and nurses risking their lives to save so many people, hearing Jason trying so hard to save them, putting so much effort into finding a cure. Maybe this wasn't just a job after all, he mused. Maybe he could actually make a difference, if he tried a little harder.

"Where are you getting the molecules? Where are the hemoglobin samples coming from?"

"Patients with RYF-2 who died. I thought if I could get a pathologist to compare a healthy versus infected liver and study the changes, maybe there would be a solution somewhere."

"Too bad none of the patients have overcome the virus," Sam mused. "Then you could try to get a blood sample of someone with a resistance. Maybe they'd have mutated Hgb molecules you could harvest. Or maybe even a biopsy of their liver, see if there is anything in there that would give you the antibody you need."

Shrugging, Sam wished his boss luck and rose, going back to his regular duties. Jason, though, stared after him, lips parting in surprise as his mind raced with the possibilities of the tech's words and he wondered how he could have possibly missed it before.

There was someone with a resistance to RYF-2. There was a flow of blood able to be utilized for a cure to the Resurrect Virus. And if that blood failed, there was a liver holding mutated Hgb molecules that could be isolated and harvested.

The only problem was, that blood, that liver, was inside his own body.

CHAPTER 24

He brought his work home that night, so much progress made, but his equation missing its most important piece. He also brought home the supplies that were currently making his heart beat too hard and his stomach clench too tightly.

For his own sanity, he began with the blood test. This was the simpler solution, the one he was pulling for because it meant a far less invasive procedure he'd have to perform solo. He sat at his kitchen counter with his arm propped up on the tile and tubing wrapped around his bicep. Flexing his hand a few times, he picked up the syringe he'd brought home and placed the tip of the needle against his skin.

"Here's goes nothing," he whispered, then pressed the needle inward with a wince. Making quick work of the blood draw, Jason removed the needle and immediately replaced it with a bandage before untying the tubing. Now he was ready for step two.

Like he did with the other dozens of tests over the past week, the sample was viewed beneath a microscope and put through the same tests, searching for the right antibodies, anything that would tell him he'd finally had a breakthrough. While he knew logistically it would take a few days to test a real viral culture, he also knew when he found his cure, he'd know instantly. The knowledge was instinctual, and it was all he had to go on.

It didn't take long for Jason to accept the truth of his draw— it didn't work. A typical blood sample wasn't strong enough, didn't hold the secrets to Resurrect Fever cure. There was only one part of his body where the blood would be strong enough. How he knew that...Jason considered it intuition, a little nugget of truth the demon tried to hide, but couldn't cloak forever.

They shared a mind now, and Jason was slowly learning how to get the answers he needed. Demanded, even.

His earlier speech to Sam hadn't been for naught. Ever since he read how to defeat the Asag, he'd known the secret to the cure lay in the liver. At first he'd suspected it to be merely the properties of the liver, trying to mimic its functions in order to eradicate the virus. After all, blood was blood—what part of the body it came from didn't matter, so long as it held the right antibodies.

Except, *his* blood wasn't just blood, and where it came from *did* matter. If the only way to kill the demon was with a strike to its liver, then it made sense that to kill a virus enhanced by demon influence, he'd have to pull blood from the source of its downfall.

He would have to take a sample from his own liver, by himself.

It took three hours, four beers, and a curse-filled pep talk, but Jason eventually made his way to his bedroom. He stripped the bed and placed upon it a long roll of paper he'd lifted from one of the hospital exam rooms, just in case. Next to the paper he laid out the supplies: pain pills, a numbing agent, gauze, scalpel, a large bandage, and a syringe attached to a long needle.

Sitting on the edge of the bed, Jason closed his eyes and searched inside his mind, heart, and soul for his other half. He could always feel the Asag, but lately the demon had been dormant, perhaps in protest. *I need you now*, he whispered in his mind, sensing a stirring at his claim. *I must do this, but I won't have the strength to do it alone.*

He felt, rather than heard, the acceptance. The Asag knew what was at stake—if Jason failed in what he was about to do, if something went wrong, then the demon would lose its host.

Jason sighed and removed his shirt, beginning what would

hopefully be a short and relatively painless liver biopsy by rubbing an alcohol swab up and down his ribcage. Such things were not meant to be performed on a person by that person, but he couldn't risk any questions being asked, anyone potentially trying to stop him. He hadn't even taken proper precautions by testing his blood and platelet counts to ensure his body could handle the biopsy. The only thing he had done was an ultrasound to determine the exact placement of his liver.

The numbing agent was used first, five quick and shallow shots around the area to be tested. It would help on the surface, Jason knew, but that was where the luxury would end. Normally patients were given a mild sedative; he would be fully conscious. He waited until his skin was numb, feeling the agent seep farther inside his body than usual, thanks to the power of the demon that also did not want to feel pain. Maybe, he considered, it wouldn't hurt so badly after all.

Next Jason picked up the scalpel with a slightly shaking hand. He'd already marked the spot on his side where the needle would enter after the ultrasound. Breathing deeply, he clenched his teeth and pressed knife to skin, grateful for the anesthetic that made the incision nothing more than a cold and small sting of pain. Blood welled up around the cut and began a slow drip down his abdomen, but he ignored it and set the scalpel down.

Ready to begin, Jason laid upon the paper on his back, his right arm up with his hand behind his head. In his left hand he held the syringe, needle poised at the entrance of the incision. Hesitation, and a small prickling of fear, had the needle shaking in his fingers.

"Just do it, get it over with," he ordered himself, willing his body to remain calm, fighting to keep his breath even. The demon within helped, giving him the courage to drive the needle forward, through flesh, between ribs, into the meat of his body.

The narrow tube of metal bit and chewed, a slice of cold pain cutting through his chest. Jason's breath exploded from him as he fought to remain still, pushing the needle farther as the muscles in his neck tightened, his fingers fisting in his hair, teeth grinding together. He couldn't help the garbled shout that escaped or the tears pricking at his eyes.

The needle dug deeper still.

In tune to a second shout, sharp metal pierced his liver. The tears burning in his eyes threatened to spill over, but Jason blinked them back and carried the biopsy through, retrieving a liver tissue and blood sample with a shaking hand. His heart pounded in his chest, neck aching due to the angle as he lifted his head higher to observe the syringe, his hand not of his own volition, but the Asag's.

Satisfied he'd gotten what he needed, Jason slowly slid the needle out of his body and placed it next to him on the mattress. For a moment he simply lay there holding gauze to his side, letting himself recover through heavy breaths and clenched fists. His entire right ribcage felt like someone had drop-kicked him repeatedly into a brick wall.

Five minutes passed before he was able to rise and properly clean himself up. A bandage was taped to his ribs and the materials put away, the biopsy sample safely stored. Not bothering to remake the bed, he simply collapsed upon the mattress with a pillow and blanket, and slept the pain away.

*

Four slides sat in a line on the laboratory table. Four physical manifestations of proof that Jason Waters had not only created a virus, but cured it as well.

It was less than twelve hours after his self-imposed biopsy, but while those hours had granted him a medical breakthrough, they had also brought upon the hospital the worst of times. Fifty-three new patients had been brought in overnight, many more turned away and brought to another hospital. All were over capacity, forced to dedicate additional floors with their own quarantine setup. Yet another makeshift clinic had hastily been constructed in the empty parking lot at St. Peters, and was being run by the CDC in an attempt to handle the overflow and help stop the spread of the virus.

The hospital was eerily silent as Jason left the lab in search of director Gary Day, one hand holding the sore spot at his right side. He wasn't sure where everyone had gone, what happened to the many, many patients who'd been admitted prior to the outbreak, and he hoped they'd been taken care of without catching the infection. There were several empty rooms he passed, others with doors closed, a few with patients resting inside, though they looked nervous and discontent.

"I would be too," he muttered.

A trip to the top floor showed complete abandonment: offices empty, desks left in disarray, most of the lights off. He knew three of the directors were in beds in quarantine, but hadn't heard news on the others. Even Gary's office was empty, though, he noted with a breath of relief, there was a mug of coffee still steaming on the desk. Wherever he was, he'd left in a hurry, and recently. Jason had to find him.

Before leaving the floor, he took a moment to look out the window at the city he'd called home for more than half his life. This high up in the hospital, he had a good view of downtown— or what was left of it.

A city in ruin. A beautiful devastation.

The bridges were all but shut down, clogged with abandoned cars and people as they tried to cross, some still going to work, others ambling about with no direction or purpose. Homes and buildings were marked with red Xs, vandals tagging any open wall space with the goal of inciting fear. Vehicles were on fire in front of those buildings, in alleys. Barrels still burned with tar. Smoke smudged the faces of those who dared to venture outside, their faces covered with masks.

And there, just outside the hospital in an area recently gated off, a pile of bodies in black bags—too many bodies for the morgue, nowhere to bury them in time, no one willing to handle the corpses of the diseased. They roasted beneath the hot Florida sun, an attack to the senses to remind everyone that the end was near. Two men in isolation suits were patrolling the area around the bodies, doing their best to shoo away vultures and rapidly losing the battle.

"The dead become life for another," Jason whispered, for the first time wondering if RYF-2 could spread to animals should the blood and flesh of the infected be consumed. He'd never thought that part through. "Time will tell, I suppose."

Knowing he was wasting time, Jason turned from the window and rushed to the fifth floor. Despite the other three isolation floors, the bustle of activity was always where it all began, where the most bodies...patients...were resting in hopes of being healed. If any of the directors or CDC officials were still in the hospital, they would be there.

Rocking on his heels, Jason waited anxiously, watching the five floors count down on the screen above his head. A ding sounded his arrival. As soon as she elevator doors opened, he witnessed the true horror of what his plague had caused.

Any semblance of order to the quarantine zone had collapsed. Too many patients filled too many areas of the floor, multiple people to a room, some forced to lay on blankets on the floor along the sides of the hallway. Trash bins were filled with bloody clothes, sheets, rags, bandages—red, everywhere he looked. On patients. On doctors and nurses. On the floor and walls despite the attempts to clean. He heard coughing and begging, saw eyes and ears dripping blood, smelled bodily fluids and waste and decay. Even in his nightmares he'd never felt such repulsion. It appeared as he'd suspected—patients had gone into liver failure, blood unable to clot, which meant they were bleeding out faster than the doctors and nurses could clean up.

Only the small lobby where the elevators were remained sectioned off, protected in a small way against the death on the other side. Quarantine suits were lined up along with an array of cleaning supplies. The smell of bleach was so strong in the air that it stung his eyes as Jason suited up. It felt like he was breathing fire. Fighting back a coughing fit, he finished dressing and entered the floor, surprised by how few others he saw in the same outfit.

It was easy to spot the medical staff in their bulky biohazard suits. They were few and far between, spread out through the halls and in rooms, but they were still there, still here for the patients. And yet, there were many more who appeared to be helping while completely exposed to the infection.

"Excuse me," he said to an elderly man leaning over a child as he tried to get the boy to drink a few sips of water. The man's nose and mouth were covered with a mask and he wore scrubs, but was otherwise uncovered. "What are you doing? You're not protected."

The old man rose, watery blue eyes staring straight into Jason's. There was resolute sadness there along with a hint of anger—at the illness, the hospital, the sick child at his feet. "There aren't enough resources for us all to be protected. I volunteered to help anyway. I came to help these people in any way I can, even if it means putting myself at risk."

Curiosity had Jason asking, "Why?"

"I'm an old man," the volunteer replied, glancing down at the child, back at Jason, all around the floor. "I am eighty-six years old. Been to war twice, lost my wife three years ago, raised two good sons who, thank God, moved to California and Texas after college and aren't exposed to this sickness." Relief was spread across his wrinkled, aged face at his sons' safety. "I've lived my life, doc. Now I'm here to help these people get to live theirs. If it means my time has come, then so be it. But the city needs help, and I aim to give it. We all do."

A look over both shoulders showed Jason what he'd missed at first glance—there were many elderly men and women ministering to patients, their focus more on the comfort and health of the ill than their own preservation. One woman sat on the hard tile with a little girl's head in her lap, stroking the child's hair and softly singing to her. Another man patiently stood at a teenager's bedside, feeding her one small spoonful at a time in between coughs.

Compassion even in sickness that will soon take them all, the Asag said, but Jason had a feeling it was meant to be an internal, personal thought. He could sense the demon was deeply curious and perhaps even moved, but didn't like feeling anything other than disdain toward the people and pleasure at the devastation it had wrought. The beast was disturbed enough by its own revelation that it returned to the recesses of Jason's mind.

"Mac." Finally finding a familiar face, Jason approached Dr. Williams. "Have you seen any of the directors? Gary, anyone?"

Doctor Williams barely glanced at him, his attention focused on administering medication through an IV to a young man. "Haven't seen him. Only directors I've seen are the ones in beds. CDC hasn't even been to this floor in a couple days."

"What the hell are they all doing then?"

Irritation mixed with exhaustion shone in the doctor's eyes. "For all I know, they are planning to burn the place down. I've hardly left this floor in a week, Jason. Frankly, I'm just trying to stay alive. I have no idea where anyone is or what they're doing or even how this hospital is still standing."

The response wasn't what he wanted to hear. "What are you saying, Mac?"

Finally stopping, Dr. Williams shook his head, arms out at his sides. "Look around you, Jason. We can't keep this up. Patients are dropping by the dozens, here and all around the city. At this point, they are dying in their beds at home or in the streets because they either don't want to be here, they don't realize how sick they are, or they just don't have faith we can help them. Any why would they?"

Another gesture around them, another sigh as Jason was dragged to a corner by the nurses' station. "Everyone who came in here two weeks ago, everyone in that first wave of infection, is dead, and these people here are quickly following. This virus is killing us too fast, and all the people who are supposed to make the big decisions are turning tail. The staff is leaving us for fear of bringing the infection home to their loved ones, and I can't say I blame them. Or they are essentially committing suicide by staying here and helping. It's only a matter of time before we all catch this, if we don't find a treatment soon. Rioters are threatening to burn us down. If something doesn't change, we aren't going to last. And what happens when it spreads?"

Dr. Williams didn't want an answer, and didn't wait for one. He merely turned and left Jason standing in a speechless stupor, for the demon-infested man had latched on to one part of the lecture and was unable to move on from its truth: everyone who'd been admitted in the weeks prior was gone. Which meant…his old college friend was gone. Eric's wife and little boys were gone, likely in an agonizing manner. He'd made Eric a promise, and he'd failed him.

Laughter echoed in his mind, satisfied and harsh. Jason ignored it and, in that moment, decided if there was no one around to make the big decisions, then *he'd* be the one to do so. He'd come to find a director, possibly a CDC official, to ask permission to start human trials, but now he'd found his answer.

The trials would start right now.

At the end of the long hallway, Jason found a room with five patients. A quick glance at their chart showed two were sisters, two more a married couple, and one individual woman unrelated to either pair. All five lay in blood-stained beds, though only three were hooked up to machines. They were clearly far along in the virus infection, their skin puckered and sickly yellow, bodies gaunt, blood caked around every orifice.

All were unconscious and took no note of his presence. Closing the door, Jason made quick work of administering the antidote. To the three on machines, he inserted his treatment via IV. To the other two, directly into their veins. In his lab it had taken mere minutes to see the effect on the virus in a small blood sample. On these patients, it would take hours, possibly days, and several more treatments he'd have to deliver in secret.

For now, all he could do was wait.

*

A smile crossed the Will O'Wisp's face, such a rare sight the three flickering flames dimmed in confusion before flashing brightly, angrily. But nothing, not their fury, not the chaos of the city, could dampen its spirits.

It watched, pleased, as Jason Waters treated patients using a cure he'd crafted of his own body and blood. He'd used his own knowledge and ingenuity to defeat the demon, even if that demon still lived and breathed inside the man's body.

The Will O'Wisp had hoped Jason would be strong enough to fight. For once in its long life, hope did not prove futile. Demon and man would, could, co-exist, bringing disorder to the people, madness to the world, pandemonium to the hearts of the many. The spirit could already see it—new diseases introduced to the nations, old sicknesses believed to be destroyed brought back with a vengeance. There was no fun in current viruses and bacteria; no one was afraid of what already had an active cure.

But, the Will O'Wisp considered as it watched the future play out before its eyes, while there would be disease, there would also be healing. A co-existence bonded by two needs—to watch the innocent suffer in sickness, and to have the world at its knees before the one who cured them.

Ego was a powerful thing, it thought, watching the happenings of the city from the window. Powerful. Unrelenting.

Destructive.

Yes, there would be death, it knew, already accepting a fate to come. But there would also be hope, and with hope, the world would always survive.

CHAPTER 25

"Jason! *Jason!*"

A frantic voice cut into Jason's dreamless sleep, causing his head to snap up from where it had landed on his desk just a few short hours ago. It took him a moment to get his bearings and remember where he was. Hospital. Fifth floor; no, his office in the lab. Five patients with a new antidote that would either heal them, do nothing at all…or kill them. A treatment with human trials not approved by the board, the CDC, or any FDA certification.

Blinking the sleep away, his eyes finally landed on Sam, who was rapping on his desk and standing next to the man previously MIA the day before. "Gary," Jason said in surprise, bypassing his intern completely. He rose and crossed his arms in preparation of a defense.

"Is…Did something happen?" He'd nearly asked if everything was okay, before realizing nothing about this city, this hospital, was all right.

Jason had been expecting the man to sigh, or shake his head, or look dejected and hopeless. He was even prepared for the police to swarm his office and arrest him for performing unsanctioned tests on patients who never gave consent. So he was shocked when Gary smiled.

"Yes, something happened, and we can't figure out if it's a miracle, a fluke, or something else," was his response around a grin and hands clasped in near-giddiness. "Five patients in advanced stages of RYF-2 began showing signs of improvement this morning. Skin color almost normal, improved blood loss and actual clotting to stop the external bleeding, and organ breakdown almost nil compared to where they were yesterday, which was complete body shutdown."

The news was a balm of joy to Jason's otherwise darkened heart and soul. He'd visited those five patients three times over the night, administering more medication but seeing no signs of healing. Time, it seemed, was what they needed. He could only hope time was enough.

"Do doctors think they'll make it?"

"It's too soon to tell if they will make it, or what kind of lasting health problems we're looking at, but doctors are hopeful." Noting the expression on the lab manager's face, Gary nodded over at Sam, an obvious dismissal, then entered the office and closed the door behind him. "Jason, before anyone else gets involved, I need to know what you know about this."

The truth was on the tip of his tongue, the need for credit and praise, but it was dangerous to admit what he'd done just yet. There was too much at stake, too much still to prove with the five patients at the end of the fifth floor hall. Plus, while he respected Gary as a doctor and a man, he was still a hospital director. What information he could be trusted with was questionable.

Testing the waters, Jason asked, "How much do you truly *want* to know, and what do you *need* to know?"

Unspoken truths passed between the two men, one not able to admit what he'd done but willing to let innuendo do it for him, the other realizing some things needed to be kept unsaid and accepting innuendo if it meant saving lives—for now, anyway. There was no time for protocol. Dozens of lives were in their hands, and there was a virus to kill before it spread to other parts of the state, possibly the country.

Deciding not to press the facts of what happened last night, Gary leaned over, hands pressed against the desk. "Do you have more?"

Now, Jason smiled. He'd been up all night manufacturing his yet-to-be-named cure, forced to take another larger blood sample from his liver now that he knew it actually worked. This time more painful, but easier, having known what to expect. "Enough for one dose for each patient in this hospital. I can manufacture more, but will need to gather the staff for help."

"Do what you need to do." Relief was clear in the director's expression. "We will back you, give you whatever resources you need."

"No questions asked?"

Now Gary did hesitate, only able to forego so much of the truth. He stared down at Jason, whose face was free of suspicion, filled only with an eagerness to get started. "No questions asked," Gary allowed, "except one." When Jason dipped his head in a single nod, he asked, "How did you create the antidote?"

A quick sting in his side reminded Jason of the previous couple days. It took everything in his power not to touch his ribs where a bandage hid beneath a blue shirt and potentially give up his secret. "I had an idea about the liver, in a way enhancing its ability to filter poisons out of the body by harvesting the Hgb molecule and attaching a cure to it. Our patients are losing blood faster than we've ever seen before, which means—"

"Anemia, clotting issues," Gary finished, starting to connect the dots. Wonder filled him, amazement at what Jason had done. "If this works, if we can treat these people with little to no lifelong effects...Jason, you've changed *everything*."

Eager to get back to work, Jason replied with another nod and rose, following the director to the door. When they stepped out into the lab, Gary added, "But, Jason, just know. Once this is over and things return back to normal, you will have to answer those questions. Maybe not to me, but to someone."

"Yes, to someone."

The intrusion of a third voice had both men turning to see

Tina Burns and her associate, Daniel Millers, standing behind them, just outside the office. Both had their arms crossed. "This is a most interesting situation we find ourselves in. We have several questions, Mr. Waters," Burns continued with a lifted brow.

I'm sure you do, he thought wryly. "Questions regarding what, exactly?"

"What happened last night?" Millers cut in, moving a step in front of his associate. "The five fifth floor patients showed rapid signs of improvement compared to the rest of the patients. Five patients in one room, no difference in their treatment versus anyone else, yet that one room are all improving? Something happened, and it wasn't a miracle. We want to know what it was, and we aren't leaving until we find out."

Indignation rose in self-defense, along with a nearly unhealthy dose of fury. "You would keep me here, asking your questions, and let dozens, maybe even hundreds, of people die, all because you *think* you need answers?"

"This is not a two-sided discussion," Burns replied firmly. "We know you created something. We know you gave it to those five patients. Yet, security footage somehow miraculously caught nothing, and is scrambled for the better part of four hours. Why is that?"

The two stared at the lab manager, who knew what they were doing, what they were trying to do. What they would not succeed in doing.

"Why," Jason repeated, a calm overtaking his body, mortal mixed with immortal power. "Why is it you searched my lab, found nothing to support your accusations against me, and continued to hold my lab accountable?"

He took a step forward. "Why is it that you haven't let my techs, people who have been here from the beginning, do their jobs, and instead slink around my hospital running your own tests and using *my* lab?"

Another step, so that the next time he spoke, it was but a whisper. "Why is it you refused to listen when I came to you with a potential cure? Why is it that, even now when patients are starting to improve, you continue with your accusations instead of focusing on the important matters at hand?"

Though her glare was steady, Burns swallowed hard. "This... this is an important matter. We know you ran these tests on those patients. We won't stand for this." But her voice was quiet, unsure.

Undeterred, Jason offered the smallest of smirks before replying, "Why is it the CDC would prefer to suffer the consequences of not supporting a cure for RYF-2?"

When her eyes widened in confusion, his narrowed. A cool breeze slid over his skin as he showed her what would happen should she push her agenda against him. Patients would heal. St. Peters Hospital would be celebrated. Jason would be called a hero. And Tina Burns' name would be dragged through media mud as the woman who stonewalled the cure. Everyone who stood with her would collapse all the same. There was only one path to follow in the war against RYF-2, and any who dared to step off would fall by the wayside, never to reach the end.

"Now you see," he said in her ear, noting Millers stepping to the side, hearing Gary shuffle back behind him. "Now you see what I am capable of doing."

Dread tingled in her chest, spreading to Millers, bypassing Gary, who was already on the demon's side, even if he didn't yet know it. It was a palpable, misleading fear, one so strong it erased their doubts of Jason Waters, and instead reminded them how much they respected him, how proud they were to be working with such an esteemed scientist.

Tricky, tricky, Jason thought with an inward grin.

"Do we have an agreement?" he asked, looking from one to the other, watching the struggle in their expressions as they began to see his way, but didn't quite understand why they were suddenly so willing to give up their suspicion and self-justification. And yet, it faded away nonetheless until standing before Jason were two people ready to save thousands of lives.

"Let me show you the cure." Gesturing into the lab, Jason waited for them to turn, then closed his office door behind him.

Mr. Waters." Burns paused, all but forcing her next words in a final attempt to maintain the upper hand. "Later, when everything has calmed down and gone back to normal, we...we will have to ask these questions."

Let them ask, the Asag whispered its invitation, and Jason felt his mind working with possibilities of what would be said, how the truth could be spun in his favor. Stretches of fact, smoothing of fiction, praises for an incredible medical breakthrough...yes, let them ask, indeed.

"Come on," Jason replied to the woman's weakly veiled accusation. "We have patients to heal."

*

Instructions were delivered quickly and calmly, not allowing for any objection or questioning. There was only one job to do and no consideration given to an alternative. What remaining nurses and doctors worked on the fifth floor began administering the antidote, a handful taking a group of volunteers to the other floors.

Schedules were set for medication, a rigid time clock to aggressively attack the virus. In the lab, Jason's team worked with the CDC around the clock to manufacture more of the antivirus so the patients could be set up on a regular schedule. Though they didn't know where the original specimen came from—and knew better than to ask—all that mattered was they keep producing more.

While the others worked, Jason took a moment to visit his original five in the room at the end of the hall. The fifth floor was a little busier today, with medical staff rushing from patient to patient, room to room, trays filled with the new treatment. Most took no notice of him and focused on the job at hand, giving him ample time to observe each patient he passed.

Many of the patients looked the same, though they weren't as fitful in sleep. A couple managed to open their eyes and peer up at him. He offered a gentle smile through his mask as he passed, making his way to his destination. When he entered, the same stench of old blood and bodily fluids met his nose, but the atmosphere was brighter—the patients were awake; they were alive.

Five sets of eyes turned to him when he walked in. None spoke, but it was apparent they wanted to know who he was, and what was happening to them. He wondered if anyone had come to talk to them yet and quickly decided he wouldn't keep them waiting for explanations.

"Good morning," Jason greeted with a soft smile. "My name is Jason Waters. I run the lab here at St. Peters. I must say, I'm so happy to see you all awake and improving."

"Improving?" one of the men croaked from his bed, still weary but able to speak for the first time in a week. "What happened? I…I don't remember anything after my wife and I went to the ER."

"You were sick," Jason said simply. "Your organs were failing and you were rapidly losing blood, all of you. But, since you were admitted we have been able to identify the disease as RYF-2, a mutated form of yellow fever. We've also found a way to treat the virus, and you five were the first to be treated."

He picked up the man's chart and skimmed it. "Mr. Peters, in just a few short hours, you and your wife were no longer in organ failure, and your body began reproducing red blood cells to replace the ones lost over the last week. Simply speaking, we managed to bring you out of organ failure so your body could begin to fight the virus and produce the proteins needed to stop blood loss. We administered a second and third dose of the antidote, which continued your upward spiral. We are hopeful that this treatment will kill the virus completely."

Next to the man, his wife began to cry—real tears, clear and salty and free of blood. "So we'll be okay?"

Jason hesitated before confessing, "Right now, I'm hopeful in saying yes, you'll be okay, but this is a new drug we are administering, and a new virus that's never been treated before. It's too soon to know if the virus will be eradicated completely, or to tell if there will be any lasting damage to your organs. For now, let's be hopeful and remain positive that you will all make a full recovery."

After spending a few more minutes with the couple, Jason moved to the sisters and spoke with them in hopes of easing their concerns. They were twins, he discovered, not having made the connection before given their drastic weight loss and otherwise illness-ridden facades. With a little more life flowing through their veins, he could now see the connection, in both appearance and interactions, the way they finished one another's sentences and never let go of the other's hand.

Bidding them both a temporary goodbye, Jason then made his last stop at the lone woman in the corner of the room. She was pretty in spite of her sickly exterior, with thick blonde hair matted with blood around her temples and ears, a delicate jawline, and vivid blue eyes as tired as they were optimistic. "How are you feeling, Miss Everson?" Jason asked.

The young woman, Amelia Everson, swallowed hard, wincing. "Better," she answered with a wispy voice. "But I still feel like I'm dying."

Jason offered her a gentle pat to the arm. "You'll probably feel like that for a while, unfortunately. But we're working on making sure you never feel like this again."

"Thank you," she whispered, lips pressing together. The expression was one of annoyance, which confused the man at her side until she added, "All of this suffering and death because of that asshole."

The statement worried him and made him pause, questioning if she could truly know how the disease actually began. "What asshole?"

A heavy breath rattled out of the woman's chest. "The guy I was dating, if you can even call it that. A horrible, abusive man. He...he wouldn't let me go. I tried once, you know. But he found me." The look in her pretty blue eyes was almost begging for him to believe her, to see her not as a woman who chose to stay, but who wasn't allowed to leave.

"Every day I had to pretend to be happy and loving so he wouldn't hurt me. He hurt me a lot." Amelia's bottom lip quivered but she refused to cry. "Then he got sick at that stupid game, and now here I am."

Frowning, Jason tried to filter through the list of patients he knew about, not even bothering with the ones he didn't. "Who was he? What was his name?"

And then she said the name that caused fury to boil in his blood. "Keven Carlson."

Patient Zero. *And so the story comes full circle*, the Asag beamed inside him.

Reading the thoughts on his face, Amelia said, "I know he died. I saw it on the news. I'd gone to my mom's in Riverside after he came here. I thought it was over and I was finally free. Then I got sick." A coughing fit broke her memory. Jason helped her through it, holding her head and wiping the spittle at the corner of her mouth. Not to be deterred, she continued, "But now I think if I'm going to be okay, and this...this virus, or whatever it is, freed me from him, then it's the best thing that ever happened to me and every other woman in the world. He can't hurt anyone anymore."

The statement rang loud and true in Jason's mind. She was so resolute in her conviction, so happy despite nearly being on death's door. In some strange, twisted way, he was proud of his plague just by her words alone. He'd done exactly what he originally intended, rid the population of the vermin and wipe away their stains on the world. There were innocents in every war, but if it meant eliminating people like Keven Carlson, he would have done it one hundred times over.

"Mr. Waters?" Amelia reached out, touching his arm and waiting until he glanced down at her. "Did he suffer, when he died?"

She seeks the truth, the Asag insisted. *She embraces the darkness. Let her bask in in.*

"Yes." The single word had her eyes closing in relief and pleasure.

"Good." A second single word had him smiling and offering a knowing smile. Amelia lay her head back on the pillow and took in a deep breath. "Sucks to suck, Keven."

Unsure if he heard her correctly, the declaration said on a sigh, Jason clarified, "I'm sorry?"

"Oh." She gave a small, tired chuckle. "Just something my friends and I used to say about people we didn't like. Sucks to suck."

"That it does." Providing Amelia with a final pat on the shoulder, Jason took his leave, walking through the halls and peering in rooms to watch doctors and nurses treat patients with the cure he had created. It would be some time before any improvement could be seen, but, in this moment, he was content knowing he'd done the impossible.

He'd created a disease, cultivated a plague, then cured the virus—and embraced a demon that made his life worth living again.

CHAPTER 26

A tentative calm had settled over the city of Savannah. The Will O'Wisp could sense it just outside the confines of its cage. Shouts had quieted, fires put out, though small sections of the city were still sectioned off while officials continued their investigations.

The Will O'Wisp heard talk through the windows by men and women leading groups of tourists around the city in the middle of the night. Mass graves were being exhumed, millions of dollars spent to restore a fragile ecosystem tainted by diseases of old. Researchers, scientists, PhDs, so many came from all corners of the earth to discover the secrets Savannah held—how the yellow fever virus survived for so long, dormant within bones, and how it could possibly spread to the plant life, to the bloodstream of an unsuspecting tourist who happened to cut herself upon a tree.

But the Will O'Wisp wasn't concerned with the city. It would recover, as it had in the past. Jacksonville would recover, never the same, perhaps stronger than it was before. No, the Will O'Wisp cared only for one thing—the latest news report showing in its mind's eye.

"The cure for the Resurrect Virus was created at St. Peters Hospital by lab manager Jason Waters after several days and even more hours of research and development. Waters credits his formerly close relationship with Tessa Taylor as being pivotal in identifying the properties needed for the cure, having ordered a blood test soon after her trip to Savannah when she was feeling ill."

An image appeared over the anchorman's shoulder, a split-screen of Jason and Tessa.

"The blood test showed properties of the yellow fever virus, which Waters was able to replicate in order to test antibodies for a cure. In an ingenious test, Waters developed his cure using blood samples from the liver, replicating its ability to filter poison out of the body. Of his unique methodology, Waters had this to say."

The screen behind him flickered, and Jason appeared, speaking to a reporter next to him in an interview he'd granted the hour prior. "We were desperate for a cure," he was recorded as saying as he stood just outside the hospital doors. "People were panicking; the city was shut down. Nothing was working, so we had to do something radical. The idea for mimicking the liver just came to me, and I dove full force into seeing what I could develop. Thankfully, it worked, and the entire staff and members of the CDC all came together to replicate the cure in order to start administering it to the patients."

The reporter, who had been nodding along, moved the microphone to her face and asked, "Mr. Waters, you are being hailed as a hero not only for treating RYF-2, colloquially known as Resurrect Fever, but for a phenomenal medical breakthrough that will change modern medicine as we know it. What do you think about that?"

Pride shone in Jason's face, but he pushed it back. "It's an honor, but I'm not letting myself take the time to really think about it. Right now, the focus is on the patients and getting these people better. Everyone at St. Peters and the CDC deserves credit for their hard work and dedication."

His words signaled the end to the interview, and the anchorman faced the screen once more. "Medical experts at St. Peters Hospital are tentatively positive, claiming their treatment is working, but it will be a slow process, with patients potentially suffering lifelong effects of the virus. Much is yet to be seen, but for now, residents of Jacksonville can rest easy knowing hope and healing are on the horizon. And, with that hope comes order. Police have regained control of downtown Jacksonville and cleaning efforts have begun. What some are calling the darkest days of our great city are coming to an end, and we can all rejoice in the sunshine upon us."

The Will O'Wisp looked away from the vision, accepting it for what it was—a reminder that, yet again, another demon had won. Jason Waters would forever be a hero, a medical genius. Those who did not know him would worship the ground he walked upon, remember him long after he was gone as a visionary, a savior. Those who were suspicious of his methods of success had been eliminated, leaving no one to question his triumphs. And those who knew the truth were a few and select three: the Asag, who would never give up its claim on the human soul; the Will O'Wisp, the bearer of demons unable to leave its post; and Jason, the man who willingly gave up his freedom in exchange for what he deemed far greater.

The Will O'Wisp looked down to its hand. Three flames blazed brightly, angrily, demanding their souls to call home. They knew their time was coming, as the trickle effect had already begun. This was how it always happened. It took but one curious or unfortunate soul stumbling upon the flame-handed spirit, and the others quickly followed.

The Pontianak demon had followed Tessa Taylor home, and awoken the need for vengeance.

The Asag joined with Jason Waters as one, together ready to create and cure sickness.

Now there were three, and they were impatient for their own souls, anger and bitterness growing in the dark Savannah house.

Soon, The Will O'Wisp promised them, folding back into the shadows.

EPILOGUE

Downtown Jacksonville was spread out before him—the St. Johns River calm and steady, vehicles flowing over sturdy bridges as drivers made their way into work, shops opening after weeks or even months of renovations caused by riots and vandals. Life had returned to normal in the four months following the viral outbreak, or as normal as possible within a city ravaged by disease.

Jason stood at the window, hands clasped behind his back as he remembered it all. At last count, he'd heard just over three thousand deaths total, and upwards of fifteen thousand who'd been cured. Hospitals throughout the city were still recovering, some with floors permanently shut down until further notice while cleanup and renovation crews worked. Funerals had been held, vigils and candlelight memorials organized, but the somberness settling over Jacksonville had yet to be lifted.

But, life went on.

For Jason, life went on well. Leaving the east window, he crossed his new corner office, passing his new desk, on his new hospital floor. Director, they named him, one of the hospital's leaders, a reward for his advances in medicine. They trusted him with the position of power, and he let them misplace their trust. Now he would be untouchable.

Standing at the western window, he looked out over all of downtown and into Riverside. Few people were on the streets this early, but they would be soon, those who had healed enough to brave the public. There were many who still preferred to stay home, going out only when absolutely necessary, some even quitting their jobs for fear of the virus making a comeback and attacking their loved ones. Others were forced to remain home, their bodies too weak to work long hours. Businesses suffered from those who did not yet return, either to work or to shop.

Life went on, but it was not an easy life for all.

They would recover, Jason knew, his assurance fueled by all the Asag had seen—cities broken down by disease would rebuild, families torn apart by death would bond once more. The present was no different than the past, except now they had more technology, and a greater capability to change, learn, recover.

"Yes, you will recover," he murmured, eyes narrowing at the sights before him, "and I will remind you how quickly it can all be taken away."

"*We* will remind them," said a woman behind him. Jason turned to see Clara perched on the edge of his desk, white blouse unbuttoned at the top to reveal a lacy bra beneath, black skirt hiked up her thighs. Her long legs were crossed, but she shifted when he approached, separating her knees so he could position himself between them.

"We will remind them," he agreed, sliding his hands up those thighs, tucking his fingers beneath the hem of her skirt while his eyes fastened on the curve of her breasts. In the deepest parts of his brain he knew she was but a hallucination gifted by the demon, but she was *his* hallucination, made to pleasure only him. He would never love her, but he would own her, and together they would rule the world.

"They think they are safe," Clara continued, drawing his head down to hers and locking him in a tender kiss, one that showed Jason in a flash behind his eyes the future prospects who would be groveling at his feet, begging him for a cure. Breaking apart, she said against his lips, "They think the sickness won't find them."

News reports stated the disease was eradicated. Sondacure, the RYF-2 antidote named in part after its creator, worked wonders on patients. The public mourned for the ones who couldn't be saved. The media asked why the cure took so long, but also named Jason a hero worthy of the history books. Those who survived the virus would forever live with organ damage, nosebleeds, and potential fevers, but they would live.

"They will live," Jason agreed with the thoughts crossing his mind, "for now."

Because not everyone at that fateful football game had lived in Jacksonville. Not all returned to their local homes, to their local families and local jobs. No, some made the drive home to neighboring cities, or even neighboring states, the virus lurking within them, waiting, growing, spreading within unsuspecting bodies. His virus was crafty, a living organism under strict instruction when to reveal itself.

"Soon," Jason whispered, his back to the city and his hands ripping the blouse off the woman he had claimed as his own. "Soon, you all will fall in sickness."

ABOUT THE AUTHOR

Night owl, Dorito lover, and quiet eccentric—Kristina Circelli is the author of several fiction novels that span genres, including *The Helping Hands* series, *The Whisper Legacy*, *Fragile Creatures*, *Damsel Not*, and *The Never*.

A follower of her Cherokee heritage, self-professed movie addict, and potential crazy cat lady, Circelli holds both a Bachelor of Arts and Master of Arts in English from the University of North Florida. She also heads Red Road Editing, a full-service editing company for independent authors. Her popular cultural novel *Beyond the Western Sun* is taught in middle schools, where she frequently offers talks and workshops for aspiring young writers.

She currently resides in Florida with her husband, Seth; cats, Lord Finnegin the Fierce and Master Malachi the Mighty; and dachshund, Pippin the Powerful. (Though she has not-so-secret covert plans to move everyone to New Zealand some day.)

BOOK

IS COMING

PERMUTED
PRESS

14

Peter Clines

Padlocked doors.
Strange light fixtures. Mutant
cockroaches.

There are some odd things about
Nate's new apartment. Every
room in this old brownstone has
a mystery. Mysteries that stretch
back over a hundred years.
Some of them are in plain sight.
Some are behind locked doors.
And all together these mysteries
could mean the end of Nate and
his friends.

Or the end of everything…

PERMUTED
PRESS

THE JOURNAL SERIES
by Deborah D. Moore

After a major crisis rocks the nation, all supply lines are shut down. In the remote Upper Peninsula of Michigan, the small town of Moose Creek and its residents are devastated when they lose power in the middle of a brutal winter, and must struggle alone with one calamity after another.

The Journal series takes the reader head first into the fury that only Mother Nature can dish out.

PERMUTED
PRESS

Michael Clary
THE GUARDIAN | THE REGULATORS | BROKEN

When the dead rise up and take over the city, the Government is forced to close off the borders and abandon the remaining survivors. Fortunately for them, a hero is about to be chosen...a Guardian that will rise up from the ashes to fight against the dead. The series continues with Book Four: *Scratch*.

Emily Goodwin
CONTAGIOUS | DEATHLY CONTAGIOUS

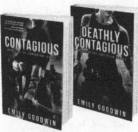

During the Second Great Depression, twenty-four-year-old Orissa Penwell is forced to drop out of college when she is no longer able to pay for classes. Down on her luck, Orissa doesn't think she can sink any lower. She couldn't be more wrong. A virus breaks out across the country, leaving those that are infected crazed, aggressive and very hungry. `

The saga continues in Book Three: *Contagious Chaos* and Book Four: *The Truth is Contagious*.

PERMUTED
PRESS

THE BREADWINNER | Stevie Kopas

The end of the world is not glamorous. In a matter of days the human race was reduced to nothing more than vicious, flesh hungry creatures. There are no heroes here. Only survivors. The trilogy continues with Book Two: *Haven* and Book Three: *All Good Things*.

THE BECOMING | Jessica Meigs

As society rapidly crumbles under the hordes of infected, three people—Ethan Bennett, a Memphis police officer; Cade Alton, his best friend and former IDF sharpshooter; and Brandt Evans, a lieutenant in the US Marines—band together against the oncoming crush of death and terror sweeping across the world. The story continues with Book Two: *Ground Zero*.

THE INFECTION WAR | Craig DiLouie

As the undead awake, a small group of survivors must accept a dangerous mission into the very heart of infection. This edition features two books: *The Infection* and *The Killing Floor*.

OBJECTS OF WRATH | Sean T. Smith

The border between good and evil has always been bloody... Is humanity doomed? After the bombs rain down, the entire world is an open wound; it is in those bleeding years that William Fox becomes a man. After The Fall, nothing is certain. *Objects of Wrath* is the first book in a saga spanning four generations.

PERMUTED
PRESS

THE BREADWINNER | Stevie Kopas

The end of the world is not glamorous. In a matter of days the human race was reduced to nothing more than vicious, flesh hungry creatures. There are no heroes here. Only survivors. The trilogy continues with Book Two: *Haven* and Book Three: *All Good Things*.

THE BECOMING | Jessica Meigs

As society rapidly crumbles under the hordes of infected, three people—Ethan Bennett, a Memphis police officer; Cade Alton, his best friend and former IDF sharpshooter; and Brandt Evans, a lieutenant in the US Marines—band together against the oncoming crush of death and terror sweeping across the world. The story continues with Book Two: *Ground Zero*.

THE INFECTION WAR | Craig DiLouie

As the undead awake, a small group of survivors must accept a dangerous mission into the very heart of infection. This edition features two books: *The Infection* and *The Killing Floor*.

OBJECTS OF WRATH | Sean T. Smith

The border between good and evil has always been bloody… Is humanity doomed? After the bombs rain down, the entire world is an open wound; it is in those bleeding years that William Fox becomes a man. After The Fall, nothing is certain. *Objects of Wrath* is the first book in a saga spanning four generations.

PERMUTED
PRESS

PERMUTED PRESS PRESENTS

INVADER MOON
Rob Shelsky

The Moon - is it a recent arrival in our skies? Compelling new evidence says this just might be the case. UFO and Field Investigator for MUFON, author Rob Shelsky, supplies convincing information that not only is the moon an invader to our skies, but those who brought the moon invaded our world, as well.

HAUNTINGS OF THE KENTUCKY STATE OF PENITENTIARY
STEVE E. ASHER

The Kentucky State penitentiary opened its heavy iron gates to the condemned over 100 years ago—yet many of them, long deceased, still walk its corridors. Noted paranormal researcher, Steve E. Asher, has uncovered and exposed the secrets of the *Hauntings of the Kentucky State Penitentiary*.

PERMUTED PRESS